Dedication

To all those who have tried to stand on skis, whether
you succeeded or not, well done!

Acknowledgments

As always, there are too many people to mention.

Natasha, you know how much I rely on you and I appreciate all the work you do for me.

Kinky Diva's – thank you for all your pimping.

Lou and Jen, love you girls and it was so amazing to have met you both this year, not just once but twice.

Samantha, there are not enough words to use to say thank you for everything.

Summer, I never realised how much of a rollercoaster ride I was going to take when I first started chatting with you. Who knew my life would change so much?

Glossary

Base: The main area at the bottom of a ski resort.

Dump: Slang for an epic snowfall of fresh snow

Off-piste: Out-of-bounds. Off a trail and other areas not marked on trail map.

Bunny Slope: An easy and flat area for beginner's.

Chatter: The vibration of skis caused by traveling at high speeds and the inability to stay in total control.

Après-Ski: The day's over – time for drinks and swapping war stories from the slopes.

Brain Bucket: Slang term for a helmet.

Camber: The upward curvature in the base of a ski or snowboard.

Avalanche Control: The triggering of

avalanches through artificial means, including controlled explosions, to make slopes safe for skiers.

Black Diamond: Expert trail denoted on trail maps and signs by a black diamond. The trail may be tricky or insanely difficult. A double black diamond indicates the steepest, most difficult runs at a resort.

Binding: What connects a ski boot to the actual ski itself. Ski bindings are designed to release from the ski during a fall.

PROLOGUE

"Oh my god. Quick someone call 999. She's hurt herself, we need to get a stretcher up here." I look around at the other women just standing there looking at me. No one is doing anything. "Please girls, this is serious!"

Finally, Kat reaches into her pocket and takes out her phone. She keeps pointing it up at the sun in different directions. What the hell is she doing?

I can hear Sydney giggling. "It's not funny! Why are you laughing? Arianna is hurt!" Molly starts laughing and so does India. "Girls, seriously. It's NOT funny! What if we can't get a stretcher to bring her down? We can't carry her." I can feel the tears coming to my eyes.

"Hello … hello … can we get some first aid up the mountain please?" I can hear Kat shouting into her phone. "Where are we? Are you having a laugh? It's a mountain! There are no road signs up here."

The giggling gets worse! What is wrong with these girls? This feels like a comedy of errors.

"We came down the yellow run, she went over one of those bump things and then fell down. Yeah a mongrel! It looks like she is going to fall off the edge of the mountain. Please come quickly." I hear Kat giving the operator her name and phone number.

She walks over to Arianna and says, "They will be here shortly, don't worry you'll be fine." She leans over and whispers something in her ear and Arianna smiles and giggles.

"Right that's enough! What is going on that is so funny? Arianna has hurt herself and near enough fallen off the mountain and all you can do is laugh. What is going on that I don't know about?"

They all stop giggling and turn to look at me. Molly and India look like they are going to burst; Kat is trying not to smile. Sydney is the only one who looks normal, well as close to normal as these girls can get!

"Kat?" I ask with my hands on my hips.

"Arianna isn't hurt that bad Sunshine, don't worry about her. She is sick though! Love sick!" All the girls start laughing; Molly falls over because she can't balance on her skis, which makes everyone else starts to wobble.

"I can't believe you did that and you rang 999! What happens when they come up here and see that she is ok? They will charge us you know."

"I HAVE twisted my ankle you know, I won't be

able to ski down, but I'm not dying or anything Sunshine." Arianna squeaks behind me. "I just really fancy Cole and well … when I fell it seemed ideal to ring and get him to come and help me. I really did hurt myself you know.

"God grant me patience with you lot." I can't believe they did that to me. I was so worried about her. No wonder they were all laughing, they were trying to match make at the same time.

"Why did I agree to come here with you ladies? I knew there would be trouble and I just knew someone would get hurt."

"Ah Sunshine, we had to have one year where we had a Sunshine Tour to the mountains."

India says, "Yeah, Sunshine at Christmas sounded like such a fun adventure!"

Are you ready for these girls again? Do you want to see how they have fun on the slopes? If so, then buckle up and join the Sunshine Tours for 'Sunshine at Christmas.'

1 BASE

SUNSHINE

The journey to Austria was as eventful as usual for a Sunshine Girls trip! There was a lot of drinking involved and the girls nearly missed their flight from Bristol. I had decided to travel on my own from Leeds as it is so stressful looking after them all. I feel sorry for Kat though, as she ends up looking after them, but she always relinquishes them quick enough when she sees me.

It always seems to be my job to look after everyone when we are away. Not that I'm complaining because I love going away with these girls – although I think I am pushing my luck by calling them 'girls'.

If you haven't heard of the Sunshine Girls before then let me introduce you to them:

First there is me, Sunshine – I am a widow with three children and rekindled a holiday romance on our trip to Madrid last year. Fate brought us together again and I am totally and hopelessly in love with him. I can ski and can't believe they talked me into bringing them here for our adventure this year.

Next is India – she is my mum and she is as mad as a brush. She can ski as well, so I'm hoping she can help me look after the others on the slopes.

Molly is Kat's mum and India's best friend. She can't ski for love nor money, she is in her seventies BUT she is game for anything.

Kat is my best friend in the World. We have been friends since playgroup. She has a very dry sense of humour and you always know where you stand with her. She has only been skiing once and might be just above beginner level.

Arianna is an absolute lunatic! She drinks a lot; laughs a lot and parties a lot, but we love her. She went skiing a few years ago, but spent most of her time in the bar and nightclubs.

Sydney is very reserved and quiet. She has never been skiing and has been looking forward to it. Her co-ordination leaves a lot to be desired though.

Now that you have met the Sunshine girls, I can continue with our story.

We organised this year's trip for December instead of October because Arianna's mum has been sick and she has been caring for her. She didn't want to come along, but we said everyone comes or no one goes. Her brother is looking after her mum for the duration of her trip away, under duress. He hasn't helped her much so he owes her this time away. She needs a break, she has spent the last six months not going out and dedicating all her spare time to her mum.

By the time the girls get to Innsbruck Airport they are sozzled and giggling. I've waited for them just after passport control, but I have been sitting here for a long time after their flight landed. Kat just rolls her eyes at me and says "Sorry Sunshine. I'm happy to hand them over to you now. I can't deal with them anymore!"

"Why, what happened this time?"

"When we checked in Sydney's bag broke, but they wouldn't give her anything to fix it." Kat says.

Sydney starts waving her arms around, getting very animated as she says "The girl was getting quite annoyed with me, Sunshine. So I took my belt off my jeans and wrapped it around the bag. She wouldn't even let me go and get it shrink wrapped, the stupid cow."

"OK, well that was good then that you used your belt!"

Arianna starts laughing, "Well not really, was it Sydney?"

"Stop Arianna, it wasn't funny."

"What happened next, Sydney?" I ask, worrying

about what is coming next.

Arianna can't speak, she is laughing so much. Sydney is bright red in the face. Kat takes a deep breath and says, "So … When we went to get our bags from the carousel, Sydney's bag came up first, and second, and third, and … and …" Kat doubles over in fits of laughter.

"I'm confused! Tell me!" These girls are killing me, making me wait for the punch line.

"My knickers were all over the conveyor belt, Sunshine. It was so embarrassing." Sydney is so embarrassed and everyone else is laughing.

I hear a squeak. "Well thank god it wasn't my underwear Sydney, someone might have thought it was a new type of backpack or something." Molly says with tears rolling down her face. Thankfully this makes Sydney laugh as well.

"That's not all though Sunshine." Kat says shaking her head. "I had to put up with these girls all morning and god forbid me but it was hard."

"You mean there's more! You should write a book Kat." I giggle.

"India got stopped at security … AGAIN! This time she not only had two see through make up bags, but she had a couple of miniature vodkas tucked in there too. When they found it they searched all her luggage to see if she was smuggling anything else. You'd think they'd know her by now!"

I look over at her and she is smiling. "They made me go through the body scanner too, Sunshine. It was really cool. You could see everything." She starts laughing and the rest of them join her.

"Oh my god mum, when are you going to grow up?" I say laughing, because I know that if she hasn't grown up by now, she never will.

"The departure lounge has been done up and there's a roof terrace and loads of new shops. We went into this new restaurant, Cabin and had some food – it was gorgeous. Then we decided to go to the terrace bar and have a few drinks." Sydney starts telling me the story then Kat takes over.

"Molly fell asleep in the bar and we nearly missed the final boarding call, so we all had to run to catch the plane." Kat says indignantly. "It was so embarrassing Sunshine, everyone was already on the plane and they were staring at us as we ran on laughing."

"Kat, I'm really sorry that I wasn't there to help you, but you see why I wanted to come on my own don't you." I start laughing because I can just picture them all running for the plane. Not a pretty sight.

"Come on, let's go and find the resort and then we can have a look around before we have some dinner. I think you ALL need some food."

They all look at me, nod and laugh. "So good to see you again Sunshine," Arianna says coming to hug me. Before I know it we are having a group hug in the middle of the airport.

We are staying in St Anton am Arlberg near Innsbruck and the drive from the airport was beautiful. As we drive through the town we can see there are a lot of Christmas festivities being held. The town is decorated with pretty lights and there is snow everywhere. I know this is a ski resort but from someone who grew up on the South coast of England, I still get excited when I see snow. We pass the huge, festively decorated Christmas tree in the middle of the town. We drive past the Christmas Market, which is one of the things on our 'Things to do' list. The smell of coffee and spices permeate onto the bus through the ventilation fans.

The bus drops us and our luggage at the doors of the hotel, but we aren't actually staying here. We have rented a chalet on the side of the mountain, we have to check in and collect the keys from the hotel reception. We had decided to treat ourselves as it's close to Christmas, kind of like a present to ourselves.

A girl called Faye shows us to our chalet. "I'm going to be on hand to help you. I'll make your breakfast and have a packed lunch ready for you every day. I see you opted to have dinner out each evening, that's fine. I'll just make sure everything is tidied away before I leave. I'll be teaching you to ski as well as my colleague, Cole."

When we follow her to the chalet I look around and can't believe how beautiful it all is. It's like looking at a chocolate box picture, like something you only dream about. I wish the kids and Xavier were here, they would love it. If the holiday is successful, I might talk to him and suggest coming back for a skiing trip with the family. I smile when I think of him. I love him so much and I can't quite believe he is back in my life. Fate was really good to me!

Kat turns to face me, "Come on Sunshine, I know who you are thinking about. You need to catch up so we can get this holiday started." She chuckles as I smile and hurry to catch up with them all. It's cold and I can see my breath when I breathe out. It's strange because even though I know it's cold, it doesn't feel cold. I think it's because it is a dry cold and not wet like back home.

When Faye leads us to a three-storey chalet I look at the other girls. "Sorry, this isn't our chalet, we paid for a three bedroom chalet with one bathroom, not a three-story mansion."

Faye opens the door and hands me the key. "This is your chalet! It looks like someone decided to treat you to an upgrade." I look at the paperwork that she hands me and see that Xavier has paid for the upgrade. I smile; he loves these girls almost as much as I do.

"Someone will be over with your bags shortly, so

settle in and then maybe you can have a look around the town and have some dinner. The Christkindlmarkt is open this afternoon, it is really festive and you can get a great selection of really nice little gifts and there is always the Glühwein Tasting. I think that is something you ladies will enjoy." She smiles at us, she must have been listening to the stories we were telling in the bus. "It will be an early start tomorrow. I'll be here to have breakfast ready for seven thirty."

"What? Seven thirty? In the morning?" Arianna is disgusted. We snigger ... she likes her lie ins.

"Yes, seven thirty. You need to be on the slopes early to catch the good snow. See you in the morning ladies." She walks out of the chalet, closing the door behind her.

When I turn to look at the girls, they are all smiling from ear to ear and then one by one they start talking. "Oh my god, this is amazing. Did Xavier do this?" mum asks pulling me into a hug. "He loves you, you know."

"Yes he did and yes he does."

"I can't believe this place. Look at that fireplace with all those logs to burn." Molly walks over to the fireplace which is open on all sides, serving the lounge, kitchen and dining area.

The whole lounge area is open plan with beautiful wooden floors, the dining area is wooden ceilings and has a huge glass cabinet with alcohol and glasses in it. "I think I could find a different drink for every hour of our stay in here." Arianna says opening the glass door and running her finger across all the different bottles.

There is a big Christmas tree stood in the corner, by the window, in the lounge area. It is decorated in traditional red and brown decorations. It's gorgeous.

As we slowly walk around the chalet I hear Kat. "Oh my god, Sunshine come and look at this."

I follow her voice and find her in the ski room, which has all our ski's and boots already laid out for us. Through the other side is a door into what looks like a small shed. I open the door and realise that it is a sauna. "That is amazing; I can't wait to try it out." I say laughing as I look around me.

There is still more to see and I hear Sydney saying "Sunshine get in here."

I daren't tell her that I don't know where 'here' is. I follow her voice and find her in a room that has totally wooden walls and ceiling, with wooden furniture. It looks cozy as I walk in, there are lots of windows and a couple of rugs on the couch. It's only when I walk into the middle of the room that I can see it is a small library. Sydney is beside herself, running her fingers across the books with as much love as Arianna did with the bottles of alcohol.

"This is amazing, I can just imagine sitting in here reading some of these books." She reminds me of Belle in Beauty and the Beast. I turn to walk out of the door when I hear the rest of the girls going up the stairs and jumping around in the bedrooms. There are seven bedrooms; maybe we can rent some of them out while we are here.

We spend the next ten minutes picking bedrooms, they are all en suite and we decide to share rather than sleep on our own. I am with mum, of course and this time we are given the best room, the double bedroom with the big balcony. While the rest of the girls go and pick their rooms, mum and I walk out onto the balcony and look at the mountain view that we have. It is spectacular.

We are at the base of the mountain; it looks so tall and majestic from here. It is totally white with small colours moving down through it as the skiers move gracefully to the bottom. Breathtaking!

"Wow Sunshine, this is so beautiful, I'm glad we came here, it's something different to what we are used to with the girls, but I know we will have so much fun. It doesn't matter where we are, fun and frivolity will always follow."

I can hear the other girls going up the last flight of stairs and there are shouts of "Sunshine, come see this." I ignore them for a few minutes and just look at the view. It really is amazing, I take my phone and take a selfie with mum showing the mountain in the background. I send it to Xavier.

"Thank you so much for upgrading us. You really didn't need to do that. Anywhere here would be beautiful. Xx"

It only takes two minutes for me to receive a reply.

"You are welcome and you deserve it so much. Miss you lots xx"

"Miss you too xx"

"Come on then mum let's go and see what the screaming is about upstairs." I link arms with mum and we slowly ascend the stairs.

"Sunshine, come here, look at this." Arianna is beside herself, she is like a child. She takes hold of my free arm and drags me into the biggest room upstairs.

The other girls are all in there already and they are sat in the plush red seats. They all turn their heads to look at me. "Wow, is this really a cinema?"

"Yeah, it seats fifteen people and there is a list of movies we can watch too." Arianna says showing me to a seat.

"Wow, this is really how the other half live, isn't it." Sydney says sighing.

"I know, we can all dream for a few days." I say sitting there looking at the screen on the wall in front of me.

After about ten minutes of utter silence Kat says

"Right come on girls we need to get changed and go for a walk so we can look around the town."

"Yeah great idea!" I stand up and walk back down the stairs to my room, I unpack my suitcase and then get changed into something nicer than the outfit I wore for travelling.

2 DUMP

SUNSHINE

When we are all ready to leave the chalet, we close the door and lock it behind us. We have put on our ski jackets and moon boots; we have leggings on and jumpers to keep warm. As we trek towards the town we realise why everyone else is wearing salopettes. It is freezing cold, obviously, but we didn't really think it would be this cold.

It doesn't take long to walk into town and when we get there we all gasp because it is so beautiful and picturesque. Just like you would see on a Christmas Card, small shops covered in snow with their lights on and their Christmas lights twinkling.

We wander around the shops for a while, looking inside at all the little gifts that we can buy. We walk past a leisure centre which has a frozen lake in front of it and its being used as a skating rink.

"We have to go there one of the days; it will be so much fun watching you guys on the ice." I laugh because I really can't imagine Molly on the ice.

"I won't skate but I don't mind watching you." Sydney says.

"Why won't you skate? Are you afraid?" I ask.

"No, I've just never done it and I know it can hurt a lot if you fall over. If I fall over in the snow then it's not as painful."

I don't tell her that the snow can hurt too.

We watch the ice skaters for a while and then we walk off to find somewhere to eat.

We see the Christmas Market in the distance and walk over to it. The smells emanating from the stalls are gorgeous. The coffee mixed with bratwurst, cinnamon, chocolate and Christmas pine trees. The stalls are so quaint; they are like small sheds with lights and decorations.

We all manage to come away with something from the market. I bought something small for the kids and I found a pair of Christmas pyjamas which look like a santa suit for Xavier to wear. The kids will love it, I smile thinking of him wearing them on Christmas Eve.

We are all feeling peckish and find a lovely restaurant which serves Pizza; we are too excited to eat a heavy meal. It is really busy and we eventually get a table. Everyone is wearing ski clothes so we don't feel under dressed.

"They obviously don't dress up here." Arianna says

looking around her.

"I think it's too cold for 'nice' clothes here," says Sydney as the waiter approaches our table.

"Can I get you pretty ladies anything to drink while you look at the menu?" He is very good looking and he knows it. Arianna takes full advantage of it.

"I'd like a cocktail please – maybe a long and comfortable screw." She smiles up at him trying to look innocent.

He smiles back at her while he takes her order, "I'm sure you do pretty lady, although I would have thought you were more a 'screaming orgasm' type of girl myself." He moves away from Arianna and goes over to Molly. "What about you sexy lady, what would you like?" He makes a point of looking back at Arianna when he says it. She is sitting there with her mouth wide open just staring at him.

The rest of us start giggling until we just can't keep quiet anymore. "Oh my god Arianna, he really put you in your place." Kat says laughing.

The waiter smiles and takes the rest of the drinks order before walking away to fetch them for us.

After we choose our food there is a commotion at the back of the restaurant, and when we turn around we see a group of lads drinking shorts at the bar, laughing and joking.

"I wonder who they are?" India says, watching them.

"I don't know, but that dark haired guy is gorgeous," Arianna says and I swear I see her licking her lips.

We all turn to look at them and I can see six young lads and girls, Faye is one of them. She sees us looking and waves at us. The cute guy pulls her to him and whispers something in her ear. She smiles and laughs.

After we have eaten the dinner, which was absolutely beautiful and none of us had realised how hungry we were, we pay for dinner and go to the bar for a quick drink.

"Can we have six beers please?" Kat asks the barman. He smiles at her and picks up large steins and starts filling them. "Er I only wanted small beers." She tries to tell him to stop filling them, he smiles at her and then she says "What the heck, fill them up."

We each take one of the steins, hold them up and clink them together. "Here's to fun in the sun."

We look at each other and laugh "And snow!" We take the steins and try to down them in one, but it's impossible!

After leaving the restaurant we go to a bar which the barman recommended, we don't intend to stay long as we've had a long day travelling. To be honest we can't see that there would be much going on here at night. Everyone has to get up early in the morning for skiing!

The place he told us to go to is called Mooserwirt and has a reputation for being one of the best party spots in St Anton. I remember seeing it online when I was researching places to go in St Anton am Arlberg. We don't really know what to expect, but we are extremely surprised when we walk around the corner and see the pub for the first time.

"I'm not sure about this place," Molly says, stopping dead in her tracks.

"Why?" Arianna asks walking closer to the music.

"Look at it Arianna, it is packed with people."

Molly is right, there are people everywhere. I don't think there is anyone inside because everyone is drinking and dancing outside. I can see skis stood up in the snow and everyone's wearing their ski clothes, so much for all the outfits we brought with us.

"Come on Molly, I think we should go back to the chalet and have a quiet drink there, let's leave these young ones to party. It's been a long day." I can't believe I heard mum right.

"Good idea India, we can open the bottle of vodka and have a nightcap before we go to bed." Molly winks at mum.

"Are you sure you know the way back? Do you

want me to walk you home and then I can come back?" I don't really want the two of them wandering about, they have no sense of direction and to be honest, it's very dark.

"No, we know where we are going don't we?" India says linking Molly's arm.

We watch the two of them walk off towards the chalet; I just hope they really do know where they are going.

We walk up to the bar and order beers and then we walk around for a bit looking for somewhere to either sit or stand. "Look there's a table here we can stand at and put our drinks down." Sydney says and I am starting to think that she will become as helpful as Kat on these trips.

After people watching for about half an hour, we all start yawning. "It's getting late; we need to get up early in the morning." Kat says finishing her drink.

Just as we drain the rest of our drinks and start walking to the door, the group of guys that we saw earlier walk towards us and they say hi.

"Hi," Arianna says and I am sure I see her blushing.

Cute guy says "Do you want a drink?"

She looks at us, waiting to see if we will stay or not. "I'm going back to the Chalet Arianna, but you can stay if you want."

"I'll stay with you," Kat says smiling at her and looking at the rest of the group of guys.

"I'll come home with you, Sunshine," Sydney says. "It's been a long day."

We say our goodbyes and hug the two girls before we walk back to the Chalet. It doesn't take us long to get back and the lights are on so we know that India and Molly made it back in one piece.

When we walk into the Chalet we can hear a lot of giggling and laughing so we make our way into the kitchen where we find Molly and India laughing their heads off at something.

I feel like her mother sometimes, not her daughter, as I stand with my hands on my hips. "What are you two laughing about?"

They both stop and look at us, mum is trying not to laugh. "We got lost on the way back, just like you knew we would. We found this little bar though with some of the locals in it. They were so nice and we were drinking some local schnapps. It was very nice."

"I can see it was nice, I think you two need to go to bed, we have to get up early in the morning."

"Yes mum," Molly says laughing. She tries to stand up but she finds it hard. "Ooh India I think that stuff was stronger than we thought. I'm a bit wobbly." She reaches out her hand and takes Sydney's arm.

Mum stands up and takes my arm and we take the two of them upstairs to bed.

Once I have mum safely ensconced in bed I go out to the balcony and take a seat. I see there is a blanket next to the chair and I wrap that around me. I take a deep breath, it's cold.

I pick up my phone and ring Xavier.

"Hey Sunshine, is everything ok?"

"Yeah I just wanted to hear your voice. I miss you already." We haven't been apart much since we got back together and I have got used to having him in my life again.

"I miss you too, I'm sure you will have lots of fun though."

"Yeah we will, the girls have started having fun already." I laugh and tell him about mum and Molly at the local bar.

"How are the kids? Are they doing what they are told?"

"Yes they are fantastic. Don't worry about anything. It's late you need to sleep, dream of me tonight!"

"I always do Xavier. I love you."

"I love you too Sunshine."

We hang up and I sit looking out at the pitch black mountain for a few more minutes, it's a complete contrast to the view this morning when we first arrived. I go back inside and get undressed for bed.

It only takes me a few minutes before I fall into a very deep sleep.

3 OFF PISTE

ARIANNA

I can't believe I didn't go back to the Chalet with Sunshine and Sydney. I know I like to party, but I don't normally make rash decisions like that. I have to say though this guy is really good looking and he keeps looking at me like he wants to undress me. I don't mind if he does. I giggle.

"What are you laughing at?" Kat says taking a sip of her drink.

"Nothing, honestly. These guys are nice; I really like the dark haired one."

"You don't even know his name do you?"

"No and I don't want to. I feel really naughty, I'm here on holiday and I want to do something really rash."

"Just don't let Sunshine know what you are up to, she's a lot of fun, but she can be very sensible too."

"I know, I don't get to do this very often, I always seem to be looking after my mum these days." My mum is sick and for the last six months instead of going out partying every Saturday night like I used to, I stay home to look after her instead. I don't mind it, but sometimes I just want to let loose and I had decided before I came here that I was going to go mad and just enjoy every minute.

"I know hun, you're so good to her." Kat says hugging me tight. I hope she doesn't say much else because she WILL make me cry.

"Come on, let's not talk about that now, I want to forget about all of that for these few days. Shall we dance?" We both look down at our moon boots, then look at everyone else wearing moon boots and we both nod our heads and start dancing on the spot where we are. There doesn't seem to be a dance floor per se, it's just dance where you are standing.

As we are dancing the group of guys come back and start dancing with us. The dark haired guy is looking me up and down. I take this time to study him and take a picture of him in my mind. He is dark haired, obviously, it is slightly floppy on top and he has dimples when he smiles. He is taller than me at about six foot, he seems muscular and I think I can see a hint of a tattoo on his arm. Sex on legs!

He moves closer to me, I can feel the room closing in on me and my heart starts to race. "When did you ladies arrive?"

"We arrived earlier today. We had dinner as soon

27

as had put our suitcases away."

"That's why I haven't seen you before, I would have noticed you if you had been skiing or dancing before."

"Oh my god is that your chat up line?" I start laughing; do people really say things like that these days?

He laughs too, thank god. "Yeah it is, don't you like it?"

"I'm sure it works for you, but you'll have to try harder if you want to dance with me."

He smiles, he's obviously not used to being challenged. "I like you; you've got a bit of spunk."

I blush when he says that word; it brings back memories of being at school and laughing when someone talked about it. I take a drink of my beer to stop myself from laughing out loud.

"I see you like that; well I can give you a bit of spunk if you want." He wiggles his eyebrows at me.

It's all too much for me, I spit my drink out in a spray which lands all over him of course. Kat nearly chokes on her beer and has to put her drink down. She is doubled up laughing so hard.

He looks at me like he is serious, which makes it so much funnier and then he can't control it any longer and he starts laughing. "I can't … I can't believe I just said that. I feel about twelve years old."

"I know it took me back to when I was at school."

He puts his arm around my shoulder and pulls me in for a hug; he kisses me on the head. "I like you … you're different."

"Oh, I'm different all right." He leaves his hand on my shoulder and I don't ask him to move it.

'Santa Claus is coming to Town' comes on the speakers and everyone starts dancing and jumping around. We join in and the lads jump up on the tables and start dancing. Cute guy pulls me up so that I am on the table too. This is so much fun. Kat watches me for a minute before she holds her hand up to one of the other lads and he helps her up too.

"This is so much fun, I can't believe we have to be up so early in the morning, but I am enjoying myself."

"You're welcome. You're a fun girl to be around. I am working tomorrow too; I'm taking a group of old ladies for skiing lessons tomorrow."

We laugh at the picture he paints of old ladies who are larger than life and have no balance at all.

When the song finishes I say, "I think we need to go. We have to find our way back to the Chalet."

"Can I walk you back to your Chalet? I don't think you ladies should be walking back on your own in the dark." He pulls me close and whispers in my ear. "I want to kiss you. You're very inviting and I don't want this night to end now, but I know we both have to get up early."

I stare at him; this good looking guy wants to kiss me! He must pull a different girl every week. I am on holiday I suppose. "Go on then! Give me your best shot." I say tilting my head up to look at him in the eyes. I see his eyes dilate as if he is shocked that I said yes.

He smiles as he looks down into my eyes and then he slowly, very slowly leans down and very gently presses his lips on mine. It's quite frustrating because I thought he was going to give me a sloppy, tongues and all kind of a kiss.

He is still smiling as he kisses me again, his lips getting softer on my lips. With each kiss he leaves his lips on me for longer. Even his eyes are smiling, he is so infuriating.

I can't do this for much longer; we really have to go back to the Chalet. I reach up and grab the back of his neck so he can't move, his eyes widen. I smile and then I start to move my mouth on his. I hear him groan and I slip my tongue inside. He follows me and we end up devouring each other. I pull back and jump down off the table. I had forgotten we were all on the tables and everyone can see us.

Kat claps her hands and squeals when I jump down. "Nice!"

I link arms with her and say to 'cute guy', "We'll be fine walking home thank you. See you around." Then we walk off before he can say anything.

I think I hear him shouting after me, it sounds something like, "Hey Spunky, come back." I don't stop to find out.

We giggle all the way home. "I can't believe you did that Arianna. Did he taste nice?" Kat laughs.

"Oh Kat, he tasted as good as he looked. Gorgeous. I had to leave though, if he walked us home, I would have dragged him into the sauna and got hot and dirty with him."

Kat stops and then looks at me; she then pulls me closer with a tug on my arm. "I love you, do you know that? Did you see his face? He couldn't believe you kissed him first and that you just walked away from him."

"I know, I bet that doesn't happen often. He seems like the kind of guy who gets all the girls. He probably works here for the winter season and then I bet he works in Magaluf or somewhere like that as a rep in the summer. A player of players."

We giggle and laugh all the way home, it was a great night and I'm so glad we stayed out.

Once we are inside, we creep up the stairs so that we don't wake anyone up and we hug before we go into our different bedrooms. Before I open the door, I say to Kat "I wanted him to walk me home though. Is that bad?"

"No hun, there's always tomorrow." Kat says, winking at me.

"I wonder if I will bump into him again?" I say wistfully.

"I'm sure this resort isn't that big and you don't intend to be a hermit do you?"

"No I certainly don't. I'm sure he'll have moved onto someone different tomorrow, maybe I should have seized the moment." I feel a little bit let down with myself, why didn't I bring him back? Ah well, there's plenty more lads out there to enjoy the rest of the holiday with. I know that the reminder of his kiss will keep me warm for the rest of the night.

"Night Kat."

"Night Spunky," she says laughing.

I giggle and then walk into the bedroom trying not to wake Sydney up as I am chuckling to myself.

4 BUNNY SLOPES

SUNSHINE

The alarm goes off and I very slowly reach over to turn it off. It feels like I've only just gone to sleep, even though I know I slept for about six hours.

I wake mum up and then go and have a shower to wake me up properly. The shower is huge, you could have a party in here, it feels kind of lonely on my own. The water is boiling hot and I love the feeling of it cascading down over me. I can hear mum moving around so I don't dawdle and finish my shower quickly.

When I'm dressed I go and make sure everyone else is up and awake. Sydney has already woken Arianna and she is in the shower. I go to the kitchen and am surprised when I walk in there.

Faye is stood there and there are an abundance of smells coming from the oven. "Good morning Faye, what is that smell?"

"I made fresh bread for you, croissants and am just waiting for you guys to come down to see if you want me to cook a fry up for you."

"Wow, I totally forgot you were here for breakfast, this is amazing. Thank you," I say taking a seat and putting some bread on my plate. She pours me a coffee and places it next to my plate.

"So did you eat in the pizza restaurant where I saw you last night?"

"Yeah the food was really nice. We all had pizza and they were gorgeous. Then we went to Mooserwirt for one drink. It was really busy."

"Yeah it's a great spot." Faye turns as the other girls come into the kitchen. There are lots of noises about the smells in the kitchen but no one wants the fried breakfast.

"I've made you some packed lunches, I'm going to go and get ready for the rest of the day and then I'll be back over to you in half an hour to help you put your boots and ski's on. There are a few safety points we need to go through and then I will take you to the 'Bunny Slopes'.

"The what?" Molly asks.

Faye laughs. "Sorry, that's what we call beginner's slopes. It's the first place you go for your lessons."

"Ah," Molly says, looking scared.

"What's going to happen today then?" Arianna

asks, looking really tired. I must ask her what happened last night and what time they got in.

"Once we've got the gear on we have to go through the safety checks, then it's out we go. As we are just on the Bunny Slopes we don't need to use the lift, although I will show you where it is for later in the week. There is a restaurant and bar halfway up the mountain, the only thing is once you get the lift up you have to ski back down again so DON'T venture up there until we say so."

"Don't worry we won't be going anywhere near that mountain." Molly says looking very worried.

"Good, now I'll be back in half an hour which will give you time to get organized and be in the boot room waiting for me." She waves as she leaves the Chalet.

We all turn to Kat and Arianna. "So ... what happened last night after we left? Anything exciting?" India is the first to ask, she always wants to know the gossip.

"It was a great night, we danced on the tables." Kat is smiling from ear to ear.

"Really? You too Kat?" Molly says not believing her.

"Yes, mum, even me," she laughs.

"It was great fun, you should have stayed, there were so many people there and they were all there to party." Arianna says looking a bit sheepish.

"So, no other gossip then?" I ask, trying to drag it out of them, they both look like they are hiding something.

"Well we talked to the group of lads that were in the restaurant, they were really nice and they liked to have fun. Nothing else really happened." Arianna is looking at Kat when she says this.

"Ok well, if you say so. Now come on, let's get ready to do what we came here to do … Ski!" I say trying to get everyone moving, it isn't even eight o'clock.

Everyone mumbles but move towards getting their coats and thick ski socks on. We eventually all meet up in the boot room to find Faye coming through the back door.

"Great you're all here. Let's get this show on the road." Faye explains how to put the boots on … how to attach the boots to the skis, obviously we won't be doing that until we get to the bunny slope.

"This is a helmet or otherwise known as a 'brain bucket', as beginners you must wear this at all times. We don't want anyone of you having to be airlifted home with a head injury." Faye laughs as she hands us each a helmet.

"There is no way I'm NOT wearing one of those. Do you remember Natasha Richardson – Liam

Neeson's wife? God rest her soul. She had an accident and was in a coma for quite a while, she died from a head injury whilst skiing. I will definitely be wearing mine." Molly says as she tries to put her helmet on, she can't get it on fast enough. We watch her as she puts in on back to front and then tries to fasten it up. We can't help laughing at her until she realises what she has done.

After about twenty minutes we are ready to go out onto the snow, we all take the skis and poles and hold them while we walk outside. Faye walks us over to the beginner's area where we wait for our instructor. "I am looking after the children today so Cole is going to look after you, he's over there," she says waving at a lad on skis. He waves back and signals five fingers.

"He's just going to be five minutes and then he will come and show you how to put the skis on and the basics of skiing." She puts her Christmas hat on as she ski's off to find the children.

"I'm really nervous," Molly says.

"Don't be, it's like riding a bike and if you can do that then you'll be laughing." India says taking her hand and squeezing it. "You won't fall over and hurt yourself, you'll just fall over. It's bound to happen, but you won't break anything."

"Thanks India, now I am more worried."

"You're welcome!" India starts giggling.

"God I am so tired, maybe we shouldn't have stayed out so late Kat," Arianna says yawning. Mid yawn she stops as the teacher skis over to us.

I look at him, he seems familiar but I can't place him. She's smiles at him and then she blushes, I don't think I have ever seen Arianna blush in her life. Something must have happened last night that she didn't tell us about. I'll get that out of her later.

"Morning ladies," he says coming to a stop in front of us. "My name's Cole and I am going to help you with learning to ski today. So who wants to go first? Tell me who you are and whether you have skied before." He looks at Arianna; he looks shocked and a little nervous. She is standing there with her mouth open, not able to say anything, so I come to her rescue.

"I'm Sunshine and I've skied for years."

"I'm India and I've skied for years too."

"I'm Molly and I've never skied and I've never ridden a bike either." She says staring at India. We all start giggling and Cole looks confused.

"I'm Kat and I've skied a couple of times."

"I'm Sydney and I've never skied in my life,"

He looks at Arianna, who still hasn't spoken. He definitely looks nervous; I can see it in his eyes. She looks at him. She doesn't speak. We all stand there looking at her because she is never speechless.

He smiles. "So Spunky ... who are you?" What did he call her? Obviously, there is more to last night that we need to find out about.

She smiles at him and then says in a very sarcastic tone "I'm Arianna; I've been skiing before but didn't get past the bar. I'm one of your 'old ladies' that you are teaching to ski today."

His eyes cloud over as she says 'old ladies', there is obviously a story behind that comment.

"Who are you calling 'old ladies'?" Molly asks indignantly.

"I was told that you were 'old ladies' on tour and I really didn't know what to expect." He is stuttering, he looks really embarrassed.

"Don't worry about it, she knows she is old she just doesn't believe it herself." I say laughing.

He laughs. "Well if all the 'old ladies' I teach looked like you, my job would be so much better."

He is quick to reply and he is really witty. He smiles at India. Nice save!

"Ok, let's start with the first lesson. How to put on the skis."

He spends the next half an hour showing us how to get the skis on and when we finally have them on, he teaches us how to move on them and more importantly how to stop. We copy him and then he leaves us to have a little ski on our own.

It is quite comical watching Molly and Sydney who have never had any lessons, as they are like Bambi on ice. He doesn't come over to me and India as we are quite accomplished, but I notice he does spend a lot of time with Kat and Arianna.

They are doing very well considering they have only done a little bit of skiing before.

ARIANNA

I can't believe it when he turns around and I see cute guy from last night. It is just typical that I am one of his 'old ladies' that he is going to teach to ski. Does that mean he is a lot younger than me? He doesn't look it. I watch him intently when he is showing us what to do; I can see his muscles under his snow trousers.

When we split up into groups to ski on our own, he spends a lot of time with Kat and I. "So, when I said 'old ladies', I didn't know it was going to be you Spunky." He smiles, god he's gorgeous. I can feel myself getting hot with the attention he is giving me.

"No problem, they must have given us the oldest teacher for that reason." I smile to show him I'm messing with him.

He laughs. "So ladies, show me your skiing techniques." We show him what we can do and then he comes over to me and stands behind me. "Now Spunky, you need to bend your knees and lean back." He pushes behind my knees so that my legs bend and then he pulls me slightly backwards, but he holds onto me. He then takes up the same position behind me so that I am almost sitting on his lap. He whispers in my ear, "great positioning" and I can feel myself blush.

I stand up straight and turn around to look at him, but as I do I can feel that my momentum has made my ski's move forward. The only thing I can do is bend my knees and go with it. I am trying to remember everything he said about doing a snow plough stop. I can't quite remember it though. I remember something about putting the tips of my skis together, but I get it wrong and open the ones at the front and keep the back ones together, instead of the other way round.

I can hear my name being shouted out in the wind as I fly down the slope, faster and faster. Why am I not stopping? This isn't working and I can see the fence at the bottom of this very small hill getting closer and closer.

All of a sudden I am on top of the fence and I just throw myself over into the snow. My skis are up in the air and all I can do is laugh. I can't stop laughing. I'm almost hysterical.

The next minute I get a spray of snow over the top

of me and I swallow it down, making me gulp. I open my eyes and all I can see is Cole looking at me. "Oh my god Spunky are you ok?" Did you hurt yourself?" He starts touching me all over checking for broken bones.

I can't stop laughing, and he is tickling me as he has to touch me hard to feel through the salopettes. "I'm ok!"

I'm laughing so much I can't talk. He stops touching me and leans over so that his face is above mine. I don't know what he is thinking and I don't know what he is going to do, but at that moment I know what I want him to do … Kiss me.

He just looks into my eyes and it looks like he wants to kiss me too, but then I hear a voice behind him. "Cole is she ok? Do you need someone to take her off the slope?"

"It's my first aid guy," he whispers.

"No, she's fine. I'm going to help her up and then she can learn the snow plough stop all over again."

"Ok then, get her up quick and make sure she knows it before she goes off skiing on her own again." I hear him swish off on his skis.

"Sorry did I get you into trouble?" I ask, I don't want him to be in trouble with anyone.

"No, but you would have done if he had been a few minutes later." He winks at me and I know that he had wanted to kiss me. I wasn't wrong.

He helps me up and he shows me how to do the snow plough stop again and again. I eventually get it right and can manage to stop without falling over. It's lunch time and Cole calls us all over. "Now ladies, we are going to have an hour break and then we are going for a little trek this afternoon. Sunshine, India and Kat, I am going to move you up to the next level and you can go trekking with their group."

"Are you girls ok with that?" Sunshine says, always worried about everyone else.

"Yeah we'll be fine. Go off and do some great skiing."

"Fantastic! Right, now ski off to the restaurant over there and you can eat your packed lunches as long as you buy a drink in there."

We start moving away towards the restaurant when Cole says, "Spunky, can I have a word with you please?"

"Yes, of course, hang on."

"Sunshine, I'll catch up with you in a few minutes." She winks at me and smiles. I watch them ski off down the bunny slope towards the restaurant.

When I turn to face him, he is smiling at me. "Your group of friends are really nice, they are so much fun."

"You mean you were expecting lots of 'old ladies'?"

"Yeah I was. I thought it was going to be a hard morning and really boring, but when I saw you there I knew it was going to be quite fun." He moves closer to me.

I blush. I can't believe he is making me blush again, what is happening to me?

"I'm not allowed to 'fraternise' with the clients Spunky; but I want to 'fraternise' with you. What am I going to do?"

"Well you're assuming that I want to 'fraternise' with you as well!" I stand there indignant, trying not to smile. I want to do more than 'fraternise' with him.

"Well, after the kiss you gave me last night, I think you do. No one has ever affected me with just a kiss before, but you did. I have to say that it surprised me … you surprised me, Arianna."

It's the first time he calls me by my name and I like the way it sounds rolling off his tongue. Ar .. ian .. na. It's like he is deliberately saying it slowly.

"I like to be unpredictable Cole; it's one of my qualities."

"I'd like to see some of your other qualities." He smiles and waggles his eyebrows.

I laugh. "How are you going to see them if you can't 'fraternise' with me?"

"Ah, so you do want me to 'fraternise' with me!" He laughs. "I am going to do some thinking this afternoon and see what I can organise. I really want to taste your sweet lips again." He moves closer to me and whispers in my ear, "Not here … Not now … But later I will …"

I start to wobble on my skis. He is affecting me that much. He catches me. "Come on, lets go and join the others for lunch." He moves away and points towards the restaurant, where the others are waiting. All the banter has gone and I feel bereft without the comfort of his hand or his words.

We ski down to the restaurant, take off our skis and go and join the other girls for lunch.

SUNSHINE

Lunch was lovely; Faye had done a great job! She'd made us salami and salad sandwiches; there was a slice of cake that was clearly homemade and an apple. Just enough to keep us going until the next break. Once we had all eaten we put our skis back on and then make our way to the bottom of the bunny slope, where Cole takes us to the chairlift so that we can go up to the first station on the mountain.

The lift takes four at a time and we split into two groups. I go with India, Molly and Sydney, then Kat, Arianna and Cole go on the second lift. It's a strange feeling, sitting there with your skis sliding along on the ground and then all of a sudden you're being lifted into the air and your skis are dangling beneath you. I can see the drops of snow falling off the bottom of the skis and looking down makes me feel dizzy.

I can hear laughter from the lift behind us and I am so happy to hear Arianna laughing. She has been having a bad time at home with her mum being sick; she needed to let her hair down on this trip. Cole seems nice, but she has to remember he is a holiday rep and he won't be there for her when she goes home. I don't want her to be disappointed and make a point to chat to her about it later.

We are sailing above the trees and they look so small beneath us. It's a really beautiful sight; it feels like we are looking down on some Lego pieces. Breathtaking! I can see the lift leveling off and we are soon coming to our stop on the mountain. I can feel my skis are back on the ground and I know that we have to jump off before the lift continues round to pick up the next round of skiers, who are going to the next station up the mountain. The lift itself bends back to carry on to the next stop so when it starts to turn, that is our cue to jump off.

I say, "Right come on ladies, as the lift slows down we have to jump a little to get off and then we will automatically move forward and the lift will move to the right and continue up the mountain. So are you ready?"

Molly, India and Sydney all say yes.

"OK, let's do this together. 1 … 2 … 3 … GO!"

We lift our bums up from the lift and automatically as we put pressure on the skis there is a tiny slope to quickly move us away from the lift, we start to move forward. I can hear India saying, "That was so much fun." Sydney says, "Oh my god, that was such a rush." No word from Molly. I turn around once we stop and I can't see her.

I look to see did she fall over once she got off the lift.

Nope … no Molly.

I can hear laughing and look towards Arianna and Kat who are just about to jump off their lift with Cole. Arianna can't control herself laughing. "What is it?" I smile, laughing even though I don't know what she is laughing at.

She is pointing ahead of her up the mountain and when I turn I see Molly still sat on the lift. Her legs are dangling in the air and she is holding on for dear life. She is screaming. "I couldn't do it Sunshine. I just couldn't do it."

"Oh my god mum, what are we going to do now?" India is laughing so much I think she pees herself just a little.

"She'll be fine Sunshine. She'll go up to the top and then come back down again. Don't worry about her, by the time we get down the bottom she will be there waiting for us." Sydney says being really sensible.

The others have arrived by our sides and Cole asks "Do you want me to follow her up? Or I can radio up for them to stop the lift when she gets up there. The only thing is that if she gets off up there, the only way down is on skis."

"Oh my god, poor mum," Kat says, trying not to laugh.

"Leave her on the lift, she will be fine. They might have to stop it when it gets to the bottom though. Thanks Cole." Arianna reaches out and touches his arm to say thanks.

He smiles at her and then talks into his radio. When he is telling the lift operator his story we all start laughing: because it really is funny. I am sure we can still hear Molly shouting for help from somewhere further up the mountain. I hope she doesn't cause an avalanche with all her screaming!

"So, are you ready to do some trekking? Sunshine, India and Kat you can go with Matthias, he will be trekking with the next group up." He points over to a tall man who is talking to a group of skiers.

"Come on, I'll take you over myself." He says as he guides us towards him.

We follow him and he introduces us to Matthias and then he skis off back to the beginners.

"Ok let's go." Matthias says. "We are going to go down the red trail, it's an intermediate trail so it won't be all easy sailing, but you didn't come here for easy." I like his no nonsense attitude.

We all line up and then off we go, we ski along for a while before the mountain trail starts to head downwards. It is such a great feeling to eventually feel the wind blowing through my hair as I speed down the hill.

There is a turn coming up and I can see a couple of the skiers have fallen down; Matthias is helping them up so that they can continue on their journey. No one has been hurt, thank god.

Mum and Kat are keeping up with me and we are having so much fun. All of a sudden we hit some moguls and Kat starts screaming, she looks like she is losing control, but somehow she manages to get that control back. "This is so much fun. Sunshine, why didn't we do this together before. I love it."

Soon enough we are at the bottom of the slopes waiting for the others to arrive.

I can hear Arianna before I can see her, she is

screaming. I think she is going a little bit too fast, she can't control the skis enough. Sydney is behind her trying to keep up; she is smiling and laughing really hard. Arianna forgets to do a snow plough stop and bangs right into the barrier.

"If any of you laugh at me, I swear I will kill you." We all stop laughing, but it is really hard because she is just laid there looking up to the sky.

Cole skis over to her to help her up. "This is becoming a habit picking you up off the snow." He smiles and looks very happy to be taking her hand and helping her up into his arms. He whispers something in her ear but we can't hear what he says. However, the smile on her face looks like he said something dirty.

We are just taking our skis off when we hear "S .. U .. N .. S .. H .. I .. N .. E." We all look up the mountain and see Molly sitting on the ski lift as it is coming down the last part of the mountain, very very slowly. As she nears the end, we see the lift being stopped to let her get off. She jumps off and skis over to us.

"That was amazing, the mountain keeps going up and up and it is so beautiful. The temperature dropped at the top though, I'm so glad I didn't get off; but please don't make me go on that one again."

We all hug her and laugh, we love her so much.

5 CHATTER

ARIANNA

I can't believe how tired I am after all the skiing today. I don't know how anyone can go out and party after a full day of skiing. I am laid on the bed thinking about today and smiling.

Firstly, skiing is so much fun! I love it and will definitely do it again and not spend more time in the bar like last time. The feeling of the wind blowing your hair as you come down the beautiful mountain is second to none.

We have all agreed that we will rest for a couple of hours before we go out for dinner. I have gone to a room on the top floor because I know Sydney wants to sleep, but I just want to think.

I can feel myself drifting off when I hear a knock on the door. "Come in, you don't have to knock." I laugh, who the hell is knocking? These girls are never private.

"It's me," I hear and instinctively I know its Cole.

How the hell did he get in here?

"What are you doing here?" I ask as I've rolled over in the bed to lay on my front to look at him.

"I wanted to come and see you," he says, sitting in the chair by the bed.

"How did you get in? Did one of the girls let you in?" I'm surprised if they did.

"I have the master key for all the chalets remember." He's grinning like a Cheshire cat. "I get a couple of hours off and wanted to get to know you better, Spunky." He winks at me.

I laugh. "So you thought you would just let yourself into my bedroom. How many times have you done that?" I laugh. He is such a player.

"Would you believe me if I told you I've never done it before. I could be in serious trouble if you kick me out and make a fuss. I just wanted to talk to you … that's all! … I promise."

That just blew me away … if it's true. I'd like to believe it is. "So what do you want to know, Cole?"

"Tell me about you … where you live … what you do!"

I pat the bed for him to climb up next to me on the top of the covers. I roll over so that I am looking at the ceiling and he lays on his side with his hand under his head, looking at me.

We spend the next half an hour talking about ourselves. He lives in Bristol, which is a couple of hours drive from me, but I don't even believe we will see each other when we go home. For me I just want to have fun while we can. I'll be going home in a few days' time!

"Can I kiss you please?" He says suddenly. I can feel my heartbeat quickening.

"I've wanted to do it all day and I really want to feel your lips against mine again." He says softly, looking me in the eye. I can see the emotion in his eyes.

I blush and lean forward, I'm not going to make him ask twice.

It's amazing! His lips fit mine perfectly and we move in sync … like we have been kissing each other forever. My heart speeds up and it feels like I can't breathe and he is giving me the oxygen that keeps me alive. We both moan, but neither of us touches the other. Just our lips.

He pulls away first and I feel bereft … alone. Neither of us says anything, we just look at each other until I start laughing, luckily he joins me.

"That was …"

"What?" I ask him, quietly. Not knowing what to expect or even what I want him to say.

He smiles. "That was different to any kiss I have ever had." He reaches out and wipes a stray piece of hair out of my eye and tucks it behind my ear. When his hand touches my skin, I get goose bumps everywhere and I still don't know if it was good or bad for him. I only know how it was for me. Unbelievably amazing!

I look at him, waiting for him to say something else. I smile and hope that he smiles back. He does and then he leans forward and kisses me very gently on the lips again. I wait for him to deepen the kiss, but he doesn't. When he pulls back he says, "I've never had a kiss that affects the whole of my body before. I got goose bumps and a strange feeling in my stomach … What does that mean? … What have you done to me, Arianna?"

I laugh, with nerves and anticipation of another earth shattering kiss, but he just lays on his side looking at me. "I don't know Cole. I felt all of that too. I thought you'd poked me with a cattle prod or something." I say with a straight face.

He laughs and it is a beautiful sound; it is a sound that I would like to listen to all the time. That thought frightens me a little. I'm a 'free bird' soaring and swooping when I want to. I don't dance to anyone else's tune. I set the parameters of all my 'hook ups' and all my relationships. I do that to stop my heart from breaking again. It happened to me once and I don't intend to let it happen again.

"You are a very funny girl Arianna and your name is beautiful, just like you." He looks deeply into my eyes. "When are you going home?"

I sigh. "We're here for another two nights and then we are travelling home." I feel sad to think that I will only see him for two more days, but if he is willing then I want to make them two very special days. Then we can both go back to our normal lives with memories to keep us warm over the Christmas period. My own Christmas memories.

"Well then we need to make the most of the next couple of days. Do you think your friends will mind if I take you out tonight? Just the two of us! I like them, but I don't want to share you with them, they have you for the rest of the year, I only have the next couple of days." He smiles at me and I can see he has crossed his fingers. He reminds me of Cruz when he wants something from Sunshine.

I laugh. "I'm sure they won't mind me disappearing, but you will have to win them over too. We usually come as part of a package on these trips and we never split up." I know that's not completely true because Sunshine had met up with Xavier on the last trip, but that was a little bit different to my situation.

"Ok, I'll do my best to get them to like me." He smiles as he leans over again and kisses me. I could swear someone is letting fireworks off in the room; my heart is beating so fast. He very slowly pushes me down and leans over me, his lips still molded into mine. I can feel his hand touching me behind my neck and pulling me even closer to him. Although I didn't think that was possible.

Once again he is first to pull away. "Oh my god I could do that all day, every day. I don't know what you're doing to me." He lays himself back down on the bed, he is still on his front and he is looking at me. He takes hold of my hand, that is laying between us, and I can see him slowly closing his eyes.

I thought he wanted to talk and get to know me, but obviously he has other ideas and I can feel mine slowly closing too. I have a smile of my face when I drop off.

SUNSHINE

It's amazing how refreshed you can feel after a couple of hours of sleep in the afternoon. Skiing really takes it out of you. I must make sure mum and Molly are ok to go out tonight, although who am I kidding? They will be dragging our sorry asses out tonight.

I hear mum moving in the bed, so I know she is awake.

"Hey mum, did you sleep as well?"

"Yes I sure did. I didn't realise how much I needed

that rest. My body isn't getting any younger you know."
She laughs; she has more energy than I do.

"I know, I don't think mine is either. What will we
do tonight? I think we should go to The Winter Garden
in Hotel Nassereinerhof. The food looks fabulous and
we can sit and look at the mountain."

"Great idea Sunshine, you always pick the best
places anyway." mum smiles at me as she goes into the
bathroom to wake herself up.

When we get downstairs, Sydney and Kat are
already there. Kat looks at me. "Mum is coming down
soon, she is just freshening up."

"Mum too." I smile back at her. "So I was thinking
we can go to one of the hotels for dinner, it looks
amazing and the view is fabulous. What do you think?"

"Whatever you decide Sunshine, you never steer us
wrong." Sydney says smiling at me.

I walk over to put the kettle on to make coffee for
everyone when I hear someone coming down the stairs.
I can hear giggling and when I turn I see Arianna and
Cole holding hands.

Arianna sees me and quickly drops his hand, but
seriously does she think I don't know where he's come
from? She walks straight into the kitchen before the
others see him.

"Sunshine, hi." She says looking sheepish.

I smile and say "Arianna." Then I look towards Cole and nod my head "Cole."

He looks like he is going to burst out laughing. "Sunshine," he says and has to turn away from me before he self-combusts. I think it is a mixture of nerves from being caught out and just embarrassment from being caught out.

"So, I was just making coffee, do you want a cup?" I say looking from one to the other.

"I will please," Arianna says.

"No, I'm fine thank you I'm going to go, but I just wanted to ask if you mind me taking Arianna out for dinner tonight. Just so we can spend some time together before you all go home." He seems really nervous.

I laugh, "I'm not her mother, of course she can go out to dinner with you as long as she wants to." I look at her and see a big smile on her face. I take my time to really study her and I can see how the smile changes her features. I realise it is a long time since I saw her smile like that. She puts on a good front so that people think she is happy all the time, but she does it to hide the sadness which lurks beneath the surface.

"So, do you want to go out then?" He is looking at the floor, like he is embarrassed.

She smiles at him and says "I'd love to."

I walk out to take the coffees to the other girls and

leave them to make their arrangements. When I walk back into the kitchen she is stood at the door watching Cole walk away. She stands there for quite a while and then is startled when she turns and sees me there.

"Are you ok?" I ask her.

"Yeah, I like him Sunshine, but I know whatever happens between us is only for the here and now, it isn't going to be forever." She looks sad but smiles at the same time. "I just want to enjoy his company while I can."

"Well if you need to talk, you know where I am." I walk over to her and hug her.

Then I take my coffee and sit with the other girls and talk about dinner tonight and which pub we are going to go to. After about ten minutes, Arianna joins us and tells the others that she is going out for dinner with Cole but will meet us afterwards.

6 APRÉS SKI

ARIANNA

I'm quite nervous getting dressed to go and meet Cole. I know I can't dress up a lot as it is cold and snowing. I put on some nice leggings and a sparkly top, but I have to put my thick ski jacket and moon boots on. I suppose he is used to seeing girls dressed like this, but it still feels like I am going to 'muck out' a horse.

When I go downstairs, the girls are all waiting for me. It feels strange to be away with them and not going out for dinner with them.

"Are you girls sure you don't mind me going out with Cole? I can cancel him you know, you are more important to me."

"Don't be so stupid, go off and enjoy yourself. You need a break and hopefully he will put that gorgeous smile back on your face." Molly says and everyone else nods or says 'yeah'.

"Thanks, I love you girls." I can feel myself getting emotional. "I'll meet you in Mooserwirt after dinner."

They all say their goodbyes and I walk out of the door. When I step through it I see Cole on the other side waiting for me. "God you frightened me there." I say smiling.

"I'm sorry, but if you were frightened does that mean I get to hold you tight?" He doesn't wait for an answer; he just pulls me into a huge hug, like I haven't seen him for a few weeks or something. He pulls away and then kisses me very softly on the lips.

"Come on, let's go." He takes my hand and holds it tight as we walk. Well I move a bit like Bambi as it is getting really cold and the snow is extremely crunchy and slippy. We walk really slow because I'm not used to the icy snow. When we get to the town, it is so pretty. It looks like something you would find on a chocolate box. There are beautiful twinkling lights in the shop windows; the snow has been brushed up off the street so that it is up against the walls. There are carol singers in the middle of the pedestrian area singing Christmas carols. I love it.

"It's so beautiful here. How long is the season that you work?"

"I usually get here in September as there is so much to do to get the resort ready for the customers. Then everything needs to be organized for when the rest of the reps arrive in early October. Everyone goes through a rigorous training programme, even if they have worked here before."

"Wow, that's a lot more than I ever thought happened. I thought that you just come over and get on the slopes and it's a jolly for you all."

"I know most people think that we are here to party, which we are, but I love it because I love skiing and being able to show someone how to ski is so rewarding."

"How long have you been doing this job?" We are coming up to the hotel where we are going to eat. He opens the door to let me in and the first thing I notice is the heat inside the hotel.

As we walk to the restaurant I look around me, the hotel is beautiful, stylish, elegant but with a modern twist. "Wow this is so beautiful."

"I know, wait until you see the view of the mountain from the restaurant we are going to."

He still has hold of my hand as he takes me through to a restaurant which is surrounded in glass. Above us, at the side of us – wherever we look there is glass. Beyond the glass is the mountain, it is spectacular. "Wow this is unbelievable."

"I know, I just can't get enough of this view. It's tranquil and you can lose yourself in the mountain view."

He is really deep, but you can tell that he absolutely loves the mountain and skiing.

He shows me to a table in the corner of the room with glass all around us. He pulls out my chair and beckons for me to sit. "Why thank you sir!" I say laughing as I sit.

After he sits down he just sits there looking at me. "What are you looking at? Do I have something on my face or something?" I say wiping my face with my hands.

"Nothing, just thinking how beautiful you are. I can't believe I bumped into you the other night."

"So corny!" I laugh and thankfully he laughs along with me.

"Normally I would agree with you, but you really are beautiful you know."

I need to change the subject, I can feel a heat washing up my body to my cheeks and I know they are flushed. "So, you didn't answer my question. How long have you been doing this job for?"

He looks out of the window for what seems like an hour, but I know it has only been a few minutes. "I've been teaching skiing here for the last eight years. I love it and I love being here. I spend so much of my time here."

"Wow! That's a long time. What do you do when you go back to England? It must be hard to get a job that gives you the time off to come here every year."

"Yeah it is, but I manage a travel agency and do some work in a hotel in Bristol for the rest of the year."

"What about family? Where do you fit them into that lifestyle?"

"I don't." He looks me in the eye and takes my hand across the table. "I haven't met anyone who can handle the constant moving from England to Austria twice a year. It's a lot to ask someone to do."

"It is, but couldn't you leave this job and just work in England?"

He looks at me and drops my hand "No, I can't do that. This is me. This is what I do. I won't change for anyone. I want someone who will love me for who I am and what I do!"

It feels cold when he drops my hand. He is quite vehement in his opinion. Is he wrong? Should he give a little for love? Who knows, I certainly don't know what the right thing for him to do is. He isn't getting any younger and if he still wants to be a playboy when he turns forty then that's up to him.

"So, you want a woman who will change their life for you, but you won't change your life for them! That's a bit selfish isn't it?" Seriously, he needs to change his opinion or he will end up alone.

"I don't mean it like that Spunky." He reaches over again and takes my hand, brings it to his mouth and kisses it. "I just want someone to take me for who I am and not what they expect me to be. That's all."

The waiter chooses to come along at that time and takes our order. I notice Cole doesn't drop my hand, but keeps it in his while we order. The waiter looks down at our hands and then over at Cole. He smiles at him – he must be a regular.

We don't talk about his job anymore during dinner as I don't want to think of when I have to go home and leave him.

After we've finished we move out to the bar to have a couple of drinks before we meet up with the Sunshine Girls. "What do you want to drink Spunky?"

I laugh. "Ooh, do they have cocktails?" He nods his head. "Goody, then can I have a 'Sex on my Face' please?" I smile at him sweetly.

He nearly chokes, but manages to control himself. "Whatever the lady wants ... the lady will get." He winks at me and walks off to the bar. The barman laughs at him when he orders my drink, they have a little conversation and then I see him walking over with two cocktails. One for me and one for him, they are both 'Sex on my Face' cocktails.

He sits down. "I can't believe you asked me to get you this drink, but you know what? It's war now." He raises his glass to me and I raise mine to meet his. "To a fun night of dirty cocktails."

I laugh. "To a fun night of dirty cocktails."

We both take a sip and I hear myself moan it tastes so good. Over the next hour we work our way through a whole collection of sexy cocktails: - Long Comfortable Screw; Sex on the Beach; Red Headed Slut; Angel's Tit and then we ended up on a 'Screaming Orgasm.' I made him order that one and I giggled as the barman laughed at him.

It was so much fun and I realise that we haven't gone to meet the girls. "Cole, I need to go and meet the girls for a drink. I'm late. Come on you'll have to help me outside and across the snow; I bet it's freezing out there."

"Come on then, of course I'll take you to the girls, but only if I can stay out with you tonight too." He stands and holds out his hand to help me up. I take it and when I'm upright he pulls me in tight. "I don't want to let you go yet, Spunky."

I giggle. "Of course you can stay with me tonight." I look up into his eyes and hope that he noticed that I twisted what he had said. His eyes tell me that he did. He leans down and kisses me, passionately.

When he pulls away we put our jackets on and walk outside hand in hand. He holds me steady. I'm a bit wobbly and I know it's a mixture of the cocktails … the ice … and the man beside me.

We walk into Mooserwirt and see the Sunshine

Girls. They are laughing and joking. Did I miss a good night? I don't care because I had my own good night with Cole.

"Hey Arianna." Kat says, hugging me. "We didn't think you were coming."

"We got carried away with the cocktail menu," Cole says, laughing. "Arianna decided she wanted to try all the ones with dirty sounding names."

"That sounds like Arianna all right." She says. "We were just going to have one more drink and then head back to the chalet."

"We'll have one with you and then I can walk all of you home." He smiles at them and takes my hand. "What drink do you want?"

"Surprise me," I say suggestively. He smiles.

"Let me get you all a drink, shot's everyone?"

All the girls say 'yeah' and I watch him turn and walk to the bar. He is extremely good looking, even from behind and I turn to look around and I see that nearly all the women in the pub are looking at his arse. I chuckle to myself and wonder how did I get him?

When he returns he is carrying a tray full of shots. He smiles as he hands everyone a drink. He looks at them all and holds his glass up into the middle. "To the Sunshine Girls and their slippery nipples."

We all choke but hold our shot glasses up and repeat his toast. We all down the shot in one go. Molly is the first to finish her shot. "Oh my goodness, that is warm going down my throat, it feels like it is burning."

"I love that. I want another slippery nipple," says India. The two of them make a right pair.

We put our coats on and then we start the cold walk home. It is really cold tonight and has got really slippery. Sunshine is supporting India and Kat is supporting Molly, because we don't want them to break anything. As we are nearly at the chalet, Cole steps closer to me to take my hand, but as he tries to take it I slip and fall down. It's like a comedy show, he is still walking with his hand out to take mine and I am laid on the floor on my back. I don't know if it hurts or not, I just start laughing.

It takes everyone a moment to realise that I am not following them and when they turn around I am laid on the ground looking up at the sky and the falling snow, laughing. Cole rushes back to me and kneels down to see if I am ok. "Spunky, what happened? Are you ok?" He takes a quick look and sees that I am laughing, so he knows I'm not hurt. "Are you too drunk to walk?" He asks, leaning further over me.

I nod my head and smile. He reaches down and puts his hands under my legs and my back and he lifts me up into his arms. "I'm going to make sure you get home safe tonight, Spunky."

"Thank you Cole." The girls have all carried on walking once they realised I was ok. "I don't think I'll be able to walk up the stairs though, will you be able to carry me up the two flights of stairs too?"

"Well that depends on whether you expect me to leave straight away, I might need a lie down." He looks at me so intently.

I smile and nod my head "I think you might need a lie down after all that exertion. You might not be able to leave for a while."

He kisses me on the lips. "You bet I won't be leaving for a while."

He catches up with the others and when they open the door into the chalet he says "I am going to carry her upstairs if that is alright with you." He stops to wait for their reply, I wonder if they said no what he would do?

"Oh yeah, we can see she can't walk." Sunshine says winking at him.

He walks to the stairs and takes me up the two flights of stairs. I can hear the girls whispering and giggling and know that I will have to face them tomorrow morning.

When he reaches the room I had been in earlier, he opens the door with his hip and then he carries me and gently places me on the bed. "Can you get undressed or do you want me to do that for you?"

I might as well enjoy this while I can. "I think you might need to undress me and then I'm feeling cold so you need to keep me warm too. I might be in shock."

He doesn't need to be asked twice, he takes my clothes off and then he climbs into the bed next to me. I am surprised he doesn't remove his clothes, but he pulls me so that I am so close he is wrapped around me keeping me warm.

7 BRAIN BUCKET

SUNSHINE

Faye has been and prepared breakfast for us, so when I get up I can smell the coffee. I knock on everyone's door to make sure they are awake, we don't normally sleep in on these trips, but these mornings are so early and not everyone is a morning person like me.

Molly and India are the first to come down. "My head doesn't feel great this morning." Molly says rubbing her head.

"I'm not surprised the amount of vodka we had last night. These early mornings are a killer for the hangover." India says handing Molly a cup of strong, black coffee.

"Yeah, it has nothing to do with our age India." Molly starts laughing.

Sydney is next and Kat soon follows her, the only person missing is Arianna and god knows what state she is going to be in this morning. I worry about her and her fledgling relationship with Cole. She doesn't really do relationships, so I know it is only a holiday romance, but I still think she is going to be hurt. I haven't seen her looking at a man the way she looks at him. I will have to have a chat with her later today to make sure she is ok.

We are eating the fabulous continental breakfast that Faye has laid on for us when we hear Arianna coming into the room, yawning.

"Good morning, how is everyone this morning?" She goes straight for the pot of coffee and then reaches for a croissant and stuffs it into her mouth before taking a seat.

"We are all good this morning, we were just wondering if you were going to join us or not." I say smiling at her.

"Of course I am, I'm here to ski and that is what we are going to do. What is the agenda for today Sunshine?" She sits down and starts piling her plate with food. Whatever she was up to last night, she certainly worked up an appetite.

"We will be having another lesson this morning and then this afternoon we will be seeing Santa!"

"What? Why?" Sydney asks.

"It's Christmas! They have a trail with Santa at the end and then his elves will help us back down the mountain. It's an easy trail so we should all be ok."

"Sounds like fun, I can't wait to see Santa, do you

think he will let me sit on his lap?" mum says smiling at me. I know she is goading me.

"Mum, only you would ask that!"

"Actually, that's a really good idea, India." Molly joins in the fun.

"God mum, not you as well," Kat says shaking her head and laughing.

After we finish breakfast we all go upstairs and get ready for another days skiing. We meet back in the ski room about twenty minutes later. Faye is waiting for us.

"So today, I am going to be taking your lesson, Cole has to go to a meeting and won't be back until later this afternoon. Sorry ladies, you are going to have to look at my face today." She laughs.

"Oh, will he be gone all day?" Arianna looks surprised.

"Yeah he won't be back until after three o'clock. Now come on ladies let's get these lessons started."

We all follow her out of the room and make our way to the bunny slopes. When we get there Faye says, "So Sunshine, Kat and India you will be going with Matthias again. He is waiting for you over by the restaurant. We'll see you ladies later – go and have fun."

"See you later girls, have fun and be careful on the lift Molly." I chuckle as I move away from them.

We ski over to where Matthias is waiting for us. "Morning ladies, how are you today?"

"Morning, it's such a beautiful morning, we are excited to have a lesson with you today." Kat smiles at him, is she flirting with him? Must be something in the air, I chuckle.

"Good, so this morning we are going to go further up the slopes and we will be skiing on moguls and then we have a small ski jump we want you to have a go on. Before you start panicking it is small, I promise. Now come on let's trek."

He starts to move away and we follow him, I am nervous about a jump, but excited at the same time.

"I'd say it would not be the only jump Arianna has had this holiday if she were with us." Kat says laughing.

The lesson is hard, but nothing that we can't do. After about an hour he takes us further up the slope and we come down the trail and over the moguls. "This is so much fun," Kat says laughing as she goes over every bump.

When we come to a stop Matthias says "So who is ready for the ski jump?"

"Is it like the one on the TV show 'The Jump'? I love that programme, but I don't think I will be able to jump one that big." India says, clearly worried.

He laughs; it makes him so much more attractive.

He looks slightly Spanish, not the best looking guy but sallow skin, dark hair and what looks like a nice body beneath his thick, padded ski wear. "No, it's nothing like that. Come on, follow me." He skis off shaking his head and laughing.

"Obviously he found that funny." Kat says, giggling a little. I think she does like him.

We follow him until he comes to a slope that is steeper than the one we have been training on, steeper than the trail we took yesterday but not too steep to frighten us.

"Now if you look halfway down the slope you will see the jump, it is made out of snow and is not like the one on the TV." He points and we can see it.

"That looks scary," India says and we all agree.

"OK, so who wants to go first?"

Kat raises her hand. "I will, then it's over and done with." She smiles at Matthias and skis over to the top of the slope.

"Great Kat, now I want you to hold your ski's parallel and just push yourself over the edge with your poles. Keep your knees bent and bend forward." I see him wink at her when he tells her to bend forward. I giggle and she blushes.

"As you reach the middle of the slope keep your eye on the snow beyond the end of the slope and as you feel the slope turning upwards, jump! Lift your body in the air and straighten it, leaning forward. You will fly through the air and when you feel you're getting closer to the ground, bend your knees and brace yourself for your landing. The idea is to stay on your two feet and not on your bottom."

He turns towards mum and I and says "Now did you hear that as well or will I need to explain it again."

"It's ok, we got it."

"Good. Right Kat let's do this. Are you ready?"

"As ready as I ever will."

We watch her intently and I hold my breath. She pushes herself off and she flies down the slope. When she hits the jump she does everything Matthias told her to do and she is literally flying through the air. Mum has reached over and grabbed my hand. I think she is holding her breath too.

We watch her land; she wobbles a little but stays upright. All of a sudden we see her lift her poles in the air and whoop. "Woohoo, that was freaking amazing!"

We start laughing, mainly from relief that she is ok but also because we are nervous that we have to do the same. When she stops at the bottom she turns and waves at us and then beckons for me to go next.

"OK! I am doing this mum, then you have to follow me. We will be ok, it's not too high." I lean over and kiss her. God I'm nervous.

I slide to the edge and listen to Matthias' instructions running through my head. I push myself off and do what any self-respecting amateur skier would do – I close my eyes. I feel the snow beneath me and take the stance, then as I feel the slope rising beneath the skis I start to lift myself up into the air. As I am flying through the air, I open my eyes.

"This is amazeballs!" I scream as I come down to land. I am the same as Kat and wobble a little, but soon manage to compose myself and before I know it I am joining her at the bottom of the slope, where I turn to wave at mum.

Yet again I hold my breath as I watch mum do the same as we did. She looks fantastic flying through the air with such grace.

We all have a hug when she reaches us at the bottom, then it is Matthias' go and he does it with such finesse and he lands so much further than we all did.

"Well done ladies! That was fantastic and no one fell, I am very impressed. So let's do it again."

"Hell yeah," Kat says enthusiastically.

We manage to get another three or four jumps in before lunchtime, it is exhilarating and it makes me feel free. I wish Xavier was here to enjoy it with me, I will definitely suggest a family holiday here. It feels strange to be including him in our family, but he is a permanent fixture in my life now. He fits in perfectly and the kids love him.

"I bet I can guess who you are thinking about Sunshine." Kat says nudging me.

"I know, I'm sorry I miss him. I don't know how I ever got through ten years of not having him in my life, how did I move on? I can't live without him now."

"You did what you had to do to survive at the time. You did it for Cruz and the girls. It's turned out perfectly though Sunshine."

"I know. Thanks Kat, I love you."

"Back at ya babe."

"Come on, we are going to ski back down the slopes to the others so that you can have lunch and then we are going on the Santa trail." Matthias says, turning his skis to face the downward slope. "There are no jumps on the way down, but there are moguls so be careful. Let's go!"

We follow him all the way down the slopes and we are all moving faster this time, it is totally amazing and I can't believe how exciting it all feels.

When we get to the restaurant, Matthias says he will come and find us in an hour ready for the trail.

We walk into the restaurant and find the rest of the

girls are already there. "How did the jumps go?" Arianna asks, looking a little bit miserable.

"They were so much fun, you should give it a try and see how you do, you're not a bad skier you know." I say trying to make her smile.

We sit there telling them what we did and how amazing it all was. They tell us about their morning on the slopes and it sounds like they had fun too.

When lunch is over, we go back over to the bunny slopes to wait for Matthias and Faye.

I stand next to Arianna and ask her if she is ok.

"Yeah I'm fine. I thought Cole would be here today that's all. He didn't say he was going to a meeting and wouldn't see me; the last thing he did say was 'See you later'. I stupidly thought I might have meant something to him, but it looks like I should have gone with my gut instinct that he was a player."

"There has to be a good reason for him not being here. Did he stay long last night Arianna?"

"Yeah he stayed all night; he only left about ten minutes before you got up." She blushes, it's so sweet.

"I'm sure he will be here later on."

"I hope so and if not then I am going to get extremely drunk tonight. Come on let's go and see Santa." She laughs.

Faye tells us that we will be going up in the cable car to the very top of the mountain and that after seeing Santa we will have the chance to ski all the way down. If we don't want to ski then we can get the cable car back down again. We all look at Molly when she says this and she starts laughing.

"Ok, I'm not sure I will be able to ski all the way down … but let's see how I feel when we get to the top. Come on we don't want to keep Santa waiting," Molly says making her way to the cable car.

The journey up in the cable car is amazing. We are all in one car and we stand around the outside of it and look out the window at the changing views. I feel like a bird soaring over the mountain. The snow is beautiful but even more so up near the top were it is untouched. There are certain parts of the mountain which are treacherous and no one is able to ski on them so they look phenomenal.

When we get to the top we can see a little cabin which has pretty little fairy lights around the door, it is so pretty. Today it's snowing which makes it perfect for meeting Santa. There are two elves waiting at the door and they show us to the queue, they really have made this a special occasion. There are some kids who we saw learning to ski here too; it's so lovely to see them getting so excited to meet him. We let them go in first; when they come out they are smiling from ear to ear and have little presents from him.

Molly goes first and then India follows her, when they come out they are smiling from ear to ear. "He is really good Sunshine, it's like he knows us or something."

I go inside and when I see Santa I laugh … its Cole. "So this was your important meeting was it?"

"I couldn't give away the magic of Christmas now could I? Do you think she'll forgive me?"

"I think she will, but I think you might need to give her an extra special present." I shake my head, what a guy.

"I really like her Sunshine, she is really special. I don't want her to go home tomorrow; I want her to stay here for Christmas."

"That's over a week away Cole, she can't do that. She has to go home and look after her mother. Her mother would be alone for Christmas and that is something that Arianna would never do. I'm sorry."

"I know, but a man can dream, right?"

"Yeah, you can."

I leave the cabin by the other door and then it's Arianna's time to go in. I watch her walk to the door, open it and I pray it will make her smile again. I missed her smile today.

ARIANNA

Sunshine waves at me and it's my time to go in. It's a bit of fun and they all look like they enjoyed it. I close the door behind me and its dark inside. I walk towards the fairy lights and I see the big red chair in the corner and that's when I see Santa sitting there. As I walk towards him I can see more of him, the lights are twinkling and I can see its Cole.

"Hello Santa, fancy seeing you here!"

"Take a seat on my knee Arianna; tell me what you want for Christmas."

"Is this the meeting that you had to go to? The reason you weren't teaching us today? I thought … I thought you just used me and pushed me aside." I can feel a couple of tears welling up in my eyes and starting to overflow. He reaches out and takes my hand and brings me to sit on his lap.

"I told you last night and this morning that's not how I felt about you. You mean more to me than that Spunky. I knew I was doing this today and I wanted to surprise you, sorry for not telling you."

"It's ok, I just let my mind wander that's all." I feel stupid for thinking that he didn't really like me.

"I know you are going home tomorrow and I want to spend tonight with you, but I don't want to go out drinking, can we just stay in tonight? You can come to mine if you want."

"Really? You want to stay in with me, I'd love that. Can we stay at mine though; the girls would worry about me if I went to yours."

"No problem Spunky, whatever you want. I just want to make you happy before you leave me tomorrow." He pulls me close and kisses me. His kisses are hot and demanding and it makes me want him.

"You do make me happy and right now you look really sexy in that outfit." I kiss him softly on the lips and stand up. "Thank you for my Christmas present Santa."

"Ho ho ho, see you later Spunky." He winks at me.

When I walk outside the girls are all looking at me, they all realised it was him and that's why they made me wait until last. "I can't believe you didn't say anything."

"We didn't want to ruin the surprise for you." Sunshine says pulling me into a hug.

"Ok shows over, let's get down this mountain. Molly are you with us or are you going in the cable car?" I ask.

"This is my last chance to ski down a mountain so let's cross this one off my bucket list girls. Let's do this!" Molly says putting her skis back on.

This should be fun. We stop and take a photo of us stood on the top of the mountain. I just know where I want that picture in my house.

We follow Faye and Matthias over to the yellow trail. Mum flanks Molly to make sure she is ok and they ski down together.

I ski next to Kat and Sunshine skies next to Sydney just to make sure we don't fall or anything.

We chat all the way down. "So Arianna, what's going on with you and Cole then?" Kat has never been known for her tact.

"Well it's just a holiday romance, you know that."

"Yeah I remember how Sunshine's holiday romance turned out!"

I laugh. "Well mine won't turn out like that and I won't be waiting around ten years for him either. Sorry Sunshine, I know you didn't hang around waiting for him, but I don't intend to even think about him when I get home. It's not that kind of a fling."

"Ok, if you say so, you both seemed so intense last night and if the noises coming down the stairs were anything to go by, then I think you were both being intense this morning." Kat laughs, I reach out to punch her on the arm, but I miss just as I go over a mogul. I fall to one side and roll over, I think I twisted something.

"Ouch, that's really hurts." My skis have come off and I keep rolling until I bang my head on a rock at the edge of the track.

"Oh my god are you ok?" Kat is the first to get to my side.

"I'm ok, but I think I hurt my ankle."

"Oh my god, quick someone call 999. She's hurt herself; we need to get a stretcher up here." I hear Sunshine shouting at the girls. "Please girls, this is serious!"

Finally Kat reaches into her pocket and takes out her phone. She keeps pointing it up at the sun in different directions. What the hell is she doing?

I can hear Sydney giggling. "It's not funny, why are you laughing, Arianna is hurt!" Sunshine is getting madder, Molly starts laughing and so does India. "Girls, seriously it's not funny. What if we can't get a stretcher to bring her down? We can't carry her." Sunshine looks like she is getting upset.

"Hello … hello … can we get some first aid up the mountain please?" I can hear Kat shouting into her phone. "Where are we? Are you having a laugh? It's a mountain there are no road signs up here."

"We went to see Santa and then we came down the yellow run, Arianna went over one of those bump things and then fell down … Yeah a mongrel! … It looks like she is going to fall off the edge of the mountain. Please come quick." I hear Kat giving the man her name and phone number.

She walks over to me and says, "They'll be here shortly, don't worry you'll be fine." She leans over and whispers, "I told them it was you, hopefully Cole will come and rescue you." I smile and giggle.

"Right that's enough, what is going on that is so funny? Arianna has hurt herself and near enough fallen off the mountain and all you can do is laugh. What is going on that I don't know about?"

They all stop giggling and turn to look at her. Molly and India look like they are going to burst; Kat is trying not to smile. Sydney is the only one who looks normal, well as close to normal as these girls can get!

"Kat?" she asks with her hands on my hips.

"Arianna isn't hurt that bad Sunshine, don't worry about her. She is sick though! Love sick!" All the girls start laughing, Molly falls over because she can't balance on the ski's which makes everyone else start wobbling too.

"I can't believe you did that and you rang 999! What happens when they come up here and see that she is ok? They will charge us you know."

"I have twisted my ankle you know, I won't be able to ski down, but I'm not dying or anything Sunshine." I say to her smiling. "I just really fancy Cole and well ... when I fell it seemed ideal to ring and get him to come and help me. I really did hurt myself you know."

"God give me patience with you lot." She sounds exasperated. I feel bad now, but I knew as soon as they said to ring for help that Kat would use it as an excuse to get Cole to me. Then again he is in the cabin on the top of the mountain in a Santa suit, so I doubt very much if he is coming anyway.

The girls try to pick me up, but I really can't move, maybe I damaged my ankle more than I thought I did. It really hurts. We seem to wait for ages before we hear someone approaching. It's Cole and he is still dressed as Santa.

He skis right over to me and clicks the release for his boots so that he can jump off the skis in one quick move. He kneels down and starts checking me over. "Are you ok Spunky? When I heard it was you I just had to leave, I left the kids up there waiting for Santa. Tell me you're ok."

"I'm ok, my head hurts a bit where I banged it and my ankle is killing me but I'll live, honestly. You shouldn't have left all those kids up there Cole."

"Someone else will take over where I left off, it's ok. Now how are we going to get you down this mountain?" He picks up his radio and speaks to some guy down at base camp.

"Girls, if you want to ski down the rest of the way then I'll bring Arianna down, there is a snow cat on its way up to help me bring her down."

"Sunshine, I'll be fine, I promise. I'll see you back at the chalet in a while; I don't think I'll be going anywhere tonight."

"I'm going to stay with you tonight to make sure you're ok, but first I'm taking you to the medic to check you've not damaged your head and to make sure your ankle isn't broken or anything." Cole says, holding my hand. He looks at Sunshine and the girls, "I'll take good care of her, I promise."

"We trust you to bring her back to us in one piece, Cole." Sunshine says as they all get back on their skis and start making their way down the mountain.

When they have gone Cole picks me up so that I am sitting in his lap, it hurts when I move my foot, but it is worth it to sit even closer to him.

"Do you know what went through my mind when I heard the radio call? Everyone knows I really like you so they made sure I heard the message." Did he just say he really likes me and everyone knows it?

"I was so worried that something really bad had happened before I could tell you how I feel about you." He kisses me on the top of my head, then he pulls me in really tight. "I really, really like you Spunky. You make me feel things that I've never felt. You stand up to me, you don't just do things to make me happy, you just make me happy by being with me." He goes quiet for a while and I'm not sure if I should speak or not.

"Cole, I like you too. You have a knack of making me smile, a lot."

He puts his finger under my chin and brings my head up to look at him. He leans down and kisses me, it's a different kiss to the ones he has given me before, this one has a lot of meaning behind it.

"I want to ask you something, I think I know the answer, but I just have to ask you anyway."

He's worrying me now. "Ok," I say meekly.

"Would you consider staying longer? Maybe even till the weekend, I have a couple of days off and I can spend that time with you, getting to know you better." He looks at me with what can only be classed as puppy dog eyes.

I would laugh but because of what he asked of me, I can't. "Cole, I can't. I have commitments back home." I feel really bad, but I have to go home to mum, she'll be waiting for me.

"I know you do, I had to ask though. I really like you and I'd love to continue this … this relationship. I don't know how it would work, but I want to give it a chance."

I can feel the tears starting to overflow; I can't give

him what he wants. I can't have a relationship with someone who is gone for almost six months at a time. Just as I'm going to reply and tell him this, the snow cat arrives.

"We need to go, but we will finish this conversation later, Spunky." He smiles and kisses me again. He stands up, lifts me up and carries me in his arms, he places me on the snow cat while he goes back and collects my skis and poles and then he puts them into the carrier on the back.

"Ok Joey, we're ready. Can you take us all the way to the medics please? Arianna needs to be given the once over." Joey starts giggling. I join him when I realise what Cole just said.

"I thought you would be the one to give me the once over." I whisper into his ear.

He laughs and pulls me closer, then he whispers "Oh I intend to do that many times over tonight." I feel warm inside when he talks to me like that.

When we get down to the bottom of the mountain, he carries me into the medics and puts me on one of their observation beds. The doctor comes in and asks Cole to leave. He looks at me and I say, "It's ok, he can stay. I don't mind him being here." He reaches out and takes my hand.

The doctor looks down at our hands and then back up to Cole, and shakes his head. He examines me and gives me some pain killers for the pain in my head. He talks about concussion and not going to sleep for a few hours. Then he checks my ankle, it is badly swollen but not broken thank god. "I am going to bandage this up but, unfortunately, you won't be able to ski on it tomorrow."

"It's ok; I'm going home tomorrow anyway so I won't be doing any more skiing." I feel Cole's grip on my hand getting tighter.

"Ah ok, I see. Well make sure you keep the bandage on and elevate your leg above your heart to help drain some of the fluid off."

I blush when he says that as I can only think of one position I'd like to be in with my leg raised in the air. Cole sees me blushing and whispers "That's what I want too." I'm so embarrassed he knew what I was thinking.

When the doctor has finished, Cole picks me up. "You don't need to carry her Cole, she can walk but she will have a limp that's all."

Cole says, "Why make her walk when I can carry her doc?" I giggle, he sounds so chivalrous.

"Come on Spunky let's get you home. We need to elevate your leg and make sure you don't go to sleep."

"Do you think you are up for the job then?" I ask, flirtingly.

"Hell yeah! I might have to try a few times though to make sure I get it right, but yeah I'm most certainly up for that job." He smiles and carries me back to the chalet.

8 CAMBER

SUNSHINE

We are all sitting waiting for Arianna to get back; we are so worried about her. The front door opens and we all turn to look. We see Cole walking in and kicking the door behind him. He is carrying Arianna and she has her hands wrapped around his neck. They make such a beautiful couple and I am worried that Arianna has fallen for him a bit too quickly. This is supposed to be a holiday romance; I hope she hasn't got in too deep.

"How is she?" I ask, moving Molly off the couch so that Cole can put Arianna down.

"She has a twisted ankle, she has to keep it raised and she isn't allowed to ski tomorrow." I notice that while he is talking, he is gathering the cushions and placing them under her leg, which he has raised and is very gently placing it on the cushions.

"Good job we are going home then, I suppose."

I watch his face as he takes in what I said. He looks upset.

"I suppose so. There's no point in her staying because she can't ski anyway." He turns to look at Arianna and I can feel the emotion between the two of them.

Molly and I walk into the kitchen to give them some space, I think they need it. The girls are already in there and they have opened a bottle of vodka, no wine for these girls. "I think I'll have …"

"… A Malibu?" Sydney says smiling "it's already poured for you Sunshine." She hands me the glass of Malibu and coke and I take a big sip, closing my eyes as I savour the warmth of it hitting the back of my throat.

"What are we going to do about Arianna girls? I think she is going to be a hot mess tomorrow on the way home."

"Why? She knows it's a holiday romance. She doesn't expect anything more from him. She will be upset it's over but she will be fine – we will be there for her, we always are." Kat says.

"I know, but it feels different this time."

We all sit there quiet for a few minutes when Cole walks in. "Can I get a drink for Arianna please?"

"Of course you can," India stands up to go and get him a drink for her. "Do you want one too?"

"Yes please. I hope you don't mind but I said I would stay with Arianna tonight as she won't be able to go out for dinner. Can I cook for all of you tonight?"

"You cook too?" Kat asks. "You are just too good to be true." She laughs to show she is joking.

"Yes, I cook. I do it sometimes for the guests who have paid for the full service. I can go out and get some groceries and make something quick and easy if you want."

"That would be great; we would love that, thanks Cole."

"No problem, I'll just get her settled and then I'll go to the shop. Please watch her though and don't let her fall asleep."

"Half of us have kids you know Cole, we know what to do when they bang their head." India says laughing.

"I know, I'm sorry. I'm just worried about her that's all." He disappears into the lounge area and gives Arianna her drink. He takes a big swig of his and places it on the glass table. I hear him talking to her and then he stands up. "OK I'm off; I'll be back in a bit."

When he has gone we all move into the lounge. "Now Arianna, we think you have a lot to tell us." Kat says laughing.

"Oh girls, you have no idea. I don't know what to do about him."

"What do you mean?" Sydney says sitting down next to her.

"He wants me to stay for a week and spend Christmas here. I can't do that."

"He really wants that? Wow!"

"Yeah, he then asked if we could continue a relationship when I go home, but I can't do that either. I can't have a relationship with a man who lives in a different country for nearly six months a year. I need more stability than that. I would worry that he does this to a different woman ever week and I don't want to think about that."

"Listen, just enjoy your last night with him and see what happens." Molly says, always the voice of reason.

We sit and chat about the holiday and how different it has been to all the other breaks that we have had.

After half an hour there is a knock at the door and it's Cole. He comes in and takes the food out to the kitchen, he comes back in and he kisses Arianna on the lips and then goes back into the kitchen. "I hope none of you are vegetarians, I bought steak."

"No, we all like a bit of meat," mum says laughing. God trust her.

He calls us all into the dining room about twenty minutes later and then he comes into the lounge and carries Arianna in and puts her on the chair next to his.

Dinner is fun; Cole is a hit with all of us. He is funny, charming and he clearly thinks a lot of Arianna. Every now and again he takes her hand and raises it to his lips and kisses it and then he puts it back down. It looks so natural and so sweet. I really do think he likes her ... a lot.

After dinner mum, Molly and I clear the table and load the dishwasher. Cole walks in and stands in the doorway. "Thank you for including me tonight, I know it is your holiday and I have kinda encroached on it, but I really like her you know. This is something different for me; I don't normally date the girls who show up for the ski school, it's not my style. Whenever I do get in a relationship, the skiing always gets in the way. This is my life and this is what I do. Girls don't understand that, it can be tough to deal with, but I don't get involved enough for it to hurt. Unfortunately, with Arianna it's different. I've got involved and very quickly. Help me please!"

He walks over and sits down at the kitchen table with his head in his hands. We all look at each other and then Molly goes and sits with him. "Listen Cole! Arianna is a beautiful girl, she is very loving and she really likes you, I can tell. She has responsibilities at home and she can't drop them right now. She likes stability in her life and if you can't provide that for her, then I don't know what will happen to you both. I'm sorry." She pats him on the shoulder and stands up to walk away.

"What if I can provide her that stability? Do you think I have a chance then?"

"I think you would, yes, but it would have to be good to give her what she wants."

He sits there in silence for a while and then he says "Thanks ladies, it's been a pleasure." We watch him walk into the lounge where he picks her up and carries her upstairs. "Goodnight. See you at breakfast," he says as Arianna laughs.

9 AVALANCHE CONTROL

ARIANNA

When we get upstairs, Cole lays me gently on the bed. Then he comes and sits next to me. "Can we talk for a while?" he asks, nervously.

"Of course we can."

"I know I probably frightened you when I asked you to stay and I know you didn't answer me. I really want you to stay for Christmas. Can you give me Christmas with you, Arianna?"

I let the tears flow; they have been threatening to do so all evening. He has made such a great impression on me and my friends and I know that tomorrow I will lose him. "Do we have to talk about this Cole? You know I have to go home, my mum is sick and I am the only one who is able to look after her. She has to be my priority right now."

He's quiet, like he's thinking.

I continue, "Look I knew this was going to be a holiday romance. I knew that the moment I met you. … I wanted you and I needed to have you. I'm just glad you felt the same way. Tomorrow I go back to my boring life and I will always look back on these few days with you and I will smile when I think of you. You have made it so special that I will never forget it."

"Is that all it is to you? A holiday fling?" He's raising his voice. Why is he getting angry with me?

"No, but Cole I'm not stupid, I know how this works. I know that you can have any girl you want and that it always only lasts for a week max. Then the new girls come rolling in. I'm not stupid – that's why you do this job, to get the girls. That's ok, that's what you enjoy. I need more stability in my life than seeing someone for a week here and there … I deserve much more."

"I know you do Spunky and that's what I'm trying to give you. I want more too, but I can't drop the skiing. It's part of me and it's a deal breaker."

"Do we really have to talk about this now? Can we not just enjoy this last night together? I want good memories of you Cole when I think of you. All those cold nights I'm going to have, I want to remember you and how you make me feel. How you made me feel this morning … last night … and how you are going to make me feel in ten minutes time. Please Cole?"

Thankfully, he laughs. "I suppose if you put it like that then I want to give you something to remember me by, especially if it's going to keep you warm on cold nights."

When I wake up in the morning I feel a weight on my legs, "Ouch!"

"Sorry Spunky, I was really comfortable. Can I get you some water and some tablets?" He leans over and kisses me.

"No it's fine, I have some here that you left for me last night." I kiss him back.

"What time is it?"

I look at my phone. "Cole, it's nine o'clock, you slept it out. Oh no you're going to be late. Get up, Get up." I start trying to roll him out of the bed. He doesn't budge.

He's laughing at me grunting and groaning trying to push him to get up. "I'm not going anywhere this morning. I'm going to stay with you as long as I can and then I have a lesson at twelve o'clock."

"Why didn't you tell me? I was panicking then." I lay back down and look at the ceiling. Thank god he didn't have to leave, I suppose I'm putting off the inevitable, but if it means he will stay in my bed for a little while longer then I am happy.

"Arianna, please change your mind. I don't want

our goodbye to be forever. I can't believe I am begging, you've just barged your way into my heart and I'm not ready to let you go yet." He pulls me into his arms, I feel comfortable here, I feel at home. I know I'm not and I know I have responsibilities to take care of when I get home. I'll just enjoy it for a little bit longer.

"Cole, please don't. You know why I have to go home."

"I know, but can't you come back and see me next weekend when I'm off? Please?"

"I can't afford it and I need to take mum Christmas Shopping. Cole, it might be her last Christmas."

"OK, I know when I'm beaten, but you can't shoot a man for trying."

"Oh you are very trying alright." I laugh.

He leans up and looks at me, then he pulls me under him and kneels above me. "Yes I am trying and I am going to try and convince you to stay." He leans down and kisses me deeply and does everything he can to convince me.

. . . .

It almost works too!

He gets out of the bed and goes for a shower; I don't join him as I need to let him go. When he has finished and got dressed, he comes over to the bed. "Spunky, do you need me to carry you downstairs before I go?"

"No, I'll be fine; I have to manage getting to the airport without you anyway." The tears are coming to the surface.

"You know you can change your mind any time!"

"I know, but we want different things Cole."

"Come by the bunny slopes and say goodbye to me, please. I don't want this to be our goodbye. I promise I won't try to change your mind again, just come and say goodbye, give me one last time to taste your lips."

"I'll see if I have time. It will be hard for me to move around on my own, but I'll try my best ok? Is that good enough for you?" I smile at him as he leans in and kisses me like his life depends on it.

"It's a start." He says when he finally breaks away. "See you before you go." He walks out the door and leaves me with a broken heart. I did this ... I can't cry until I get home ...I need to be strong.

I eventually climb out of the bed and pack my suitcase. My ankle is really sore, but I manage to hobble about. When I finally make it downstairs the others are waiting for me. "I can't bring my suitcase down, if someone can help me that would be great."

"I'll do it for you, sit down Arianna." Sydney says helping me to the couch.

"What is going on? How are you?" Sunshine asks.

"I'm ok, I just have to think of Cole as a holiday romance and then I'll be fine. He wants me to stay or come back next weekend but I said no. I can't do that, I have mum to look after."

"He asked you to stay or come back. That doesn't sound like it was just a holiday romance to him." Kat says.

"I know it's strange I thought he would be delighted to go back to his playboy lifestyle, although he says he doesn't live that life."

"He really likes you. Would you not consider a compromise? You could do the long distance relationship thing for a while and then he will be back in the UK in a couple of months." Kat seems to want me to try and make this work.

"Yeah, but then he's in Bristol and I'm in Torquay. It wouldn't work."

"If you say so, but I know that if a man looked at me the way he looks at you when he is telling you he wants you to stay and make a go of a relationship, then I would definitely try." She comes over and hugs me. I feel like sobbing, but I know I have to be strong. I can cry when I'm home and on my own.

"Yeah look Arianna; we haven't seen you that happy for a long time, since before your mum got sick. You still need to live your life you know." She lets me go and kneels in front of me. "Sometimes you need to take a risk, especially with love. It doesn't always land in your lap; you have to work for it. If he means as much to you, as you so obviously mean to him, then do something about it."

The tears come now, I can't hold them back. "Honestly, I can't see how it will work. Maybe I should try though. Should I?"

All of the Sunshine girls answer at the same time "YES!" I guess that's my answer.

"Right, so who is going to help me to the bunny slopes to see him so that I can tell him I've decided to give us a go. I really want to make it work girls; I just didn't want to be foolish in believing he wanted me. Thank you."

Sunshine offers to take me to the slope, she helps me to put on my snow boots and then she holds me while I put some pressure on my foot. It hurts like hell, but I can manage it with her help.

It takes us quite a while to get to the bunny slope and I spend a few minutes watching Cole teaching his class of children how to ski. He looks so gorgeous in his ski wear and he is bending down talking to the children, listening to them intently.

I make a move to go and see him, when I see a blonde girl running up to him. She calls his name and when he turns, his whole face lights up. I watch them and everything looks like it is happening in slow motion.

He walks towards her and he hugs her. Then I see him kiss her, then he pulls her tight again and I can see how happy he is to see this girl. I don't wait any longer. "Sunshine, please help me back to the chalet. I was obviously right with my first impression. He's a player. That is obviously another girl he was trying to seduce like me." I am so upset, the tears won't stop.

As we are walking back to the chalet we pass Faye, who is coming out with our luggage, ready to load it up on the transfer bus. "Are you ok Arianna?"

"I'm in pain that's all. It really hurts; I just want to go home." Sunshine helps me into the chalet to find the girls. I sit on the couch and watch them all scurrying around to get everything in the bus. The last thing they take to the bus is me; they help me down the stairs and onto the bus. All the time I am crying and they don't say anything. I think they were as duped by him as I was.

The bus sets off and it has to go past the bunny slopes and I can see Cole, he is stood with his arm around the blonde who has her head on his shoulder. Seeing this sets off another round of sobbing uncontrollably. Kat sees him and starts shouting at the window. "You bastard, you had us all convinced that you weren't a playboy and you broke Arianna's heart."

I don't say anything until we get on the plane and then as we take off I say to myself, "Goodbye Cole, you're nothing more than a gigolo."

When I get home, mum is waiting for me. My brother had stayed in the house with her while I was gone, but he can't get out of there quick enough when I pull up at the door.

He leaves almost immediately; he hugs me and says "I don't know how you do it. You must have the patience of a saint." Then he walks off and leaves me with mum and my grief.

Getting ready for Christmas isn't fun this year, both with mum being so sick and with the affect Cole had on my heart. Today I am taking mum shopping for some Christmas presents. My ankle is much better, not that I've had time to rest it, but I've not gone anywhere at night times, just stayed in my room, sulking.

I feel a bit better, I had said it was a holiday romance and that is what it will always be in my mind. The fact that he wanted more is what is killing me and then to find out that he is just like every other hot blooded male and just out for sex.

Sunshine rings me while we are out shopping. "Arianna, I want you to come to mum's for Christmas Day. I know you are still recuperating and cooking dinner will be too much for you. We can all help you with your mum then. Please don't say no!"

"I've never spent Christmas day anywhere other than at home Sunshine, I don't know."

"Think about it and let me know, but the girls are going to be there too. We are going to have a big celebration."

"Ok I'll do it. It will be nice to see you all again. Thanks Sunshine."

"Listen, stop moping around, let's just enjoy Christmas."

"Thank you, it will make it so much easier." I hang up the phone and I have a smile on my face. I tell mum and after a little bit of complaining she is happy that we get to spend the holiday with our special friends.

We buy presents for them all, nothing too expensive but something meaningful. I'm starting to get excited about Christmas now. Why am I miserable? I have everything I need for a good Christmas. Family … Great friends … and some great holiday memories. I make a deal with myself not to be upset anymore, I need to move on and chalk it up to experience.

10 BLACK DIAMOND

COLE

I have enjoyed the last few days with Arianna more than anything. It is amazing how quick one person can turn your life upside down. Arianna made me feel like someone really special and important. I can't believe I asked her to stay. I never do that. I don't want to settle down. She made me want to change my life, to be the stability that she needs if it means that I can have her in my life. I'm hoping she comes over to see me before she goes; I am going to ask her one more time and tell her that maybe we can work something out. I shouldn't just expect her to change her life for me; I should change my life for her as well.

I keep looking around when I should be concentrating on the kids that are skiing. They keep clapping and I am missing what is going on, but I can't concentrate. If I could just walk out of here to go and find her then I would, but it's not that easy. These parents have paid good money for their kids to be taught how to ski.

I must have been here for about an hour when I hear someone call my name, I turn around smiling expecting to see Arianna, but no it's my little sister, Bianca. What's she doing here? She isn't due until the weekend.

"Cole, Cole," she says as she throws herself at me and hugs me tight.

"Hey Bi, what are you doing here?" I kiss her on the cheek, she is holding on for dear life and not letting go. "You weren't supposed to be here until Saturday."

"I know, I couldn't wait. I am so excited, you know I love coming out here for Christmas. mum and Dad are on their way too. Dad just had to drop into the hotel to make sure you've been looking after everything properly. You know Dad, he finds it hard to let go."

I roll my eyes because since Dad 'retired', at least that's what he calls it, he is still working loads of hours a week. I've been looking after the hotel, chalets and ski resort on my own for the last two years, before that I used to help Dad while he trained me up. During the summer I go home and run the hotel there and I helped to set up the Travel Agency, which Bianca is going to be running on her own.

We are both really lucky to have our successful parents, we have been able to live this amazing life where we travel and spend months out of the country each year. Only now I'm not sure how happy it's going to make me and it's the first time I wish I could go home and settle down.

"I knew he wouldn't be able to stay away for too long. How was the flight?"

"It was fine, you know Dad the closer he gets the more he starts to stress."

I laugh, because I know this so well and he will be stressing not only himself but the staff at the hotel too.

Bianca leaves to go to the biggest chalet, which is where I live, so that she can unpack and I tell her that I will see her for dinner later.

I continue teaching the kids but my mind isn't fully on the job, I am very disappointed that Arianna didn't come to see me before she left. I can't believe I didn't take her number or anything; I have no way of getting hold of her. 'A holiday romance' she called it, maybe its best left that way.

When I've finished for the day I go to the bar to have a drink and I bump into Faye. I can't help myself from asking "Did you help Arianna and the girls to the transfer bus this lunchtime?"

"Yeah I did, I made sure they got to the airport." She snaps at me.

"Did Arianna say anything about me? I'm so mad I didn't get her mobile number."

She looks down at the floor. She doesn't say anything.

"Faye what aren't you telling me?"

"Listen Cole, you're my boss and this is my first year working here. I like my job … a lot and I don't want to get involved in your sex life or anything so please don't bring me into it." She sounds really angry at something.

"What are you talking about?"

"I haven't seen you with any women since I've been here but what you did today was disgraceful. You broke Arianna's heart into a million pieces."

"What are you talking about Faye? I don't understand."

"Arianna came to see you; from what I overheard she said she wanted to tell you that she was willing to give a long distance relationship a try."

I gasp.

"The girls told me that was really epic for her, because of the problems she has at home. Sunshine helped her to walk over to the bunny slopes and when she got there she saw a blonde girl running into your arms and kissing you. She was devastated. She had believed your cock and bull story about having to work here and never having girls. If you don't mind me saying Cole, that is disgusting that you would have another girl

112

lined up before she even left."

She turns away in disgust and starts to walk away. "Faye, let me explain."

"Cole, you don't have to explain to me. It's Arianna you need to explain to … oh yeah you didn't get her number so you can't!"

"That blonde is my sister and she is really big into public displays of affection." I put my head into my hands. I can't believe that Arianna's last picture of me was in the arms of another girl. I can feel tears coming to my eyes, I start punching the bar in front of me. I'm so angry.

"Oh my god Cole, what … what's wrong?" Faye sits down next to me and takes one of my hands. "Please stop hitting the bar." She is really uncomfortable.

"I'm sorry. I thought she didn't want to see me again but I was hoping she did. Now you tell me she came to me because she wanted to try and then she saw Bianca all over me. What she must think of me I just can't imagine. I have no way of getting hold of her and I don't want her to think that this was just sex, it meant so much more to me than that."

Faye doesn't really know what to do or what to say to me. "Listen Cole, you are a very determined man and I am sure if you set your mind to it you can find a way." She gets up and rests her hand on my shoulder. "See you later Cole. I know you're not a bad man. I'm sorry for shouting at you, but it did look really bad."

I sit there for a long time thinking back on the last few days and how much Arianna has changed me … how she has made me want more in my life than working at a ski resort and now I have blown it. I'm devastated and I need to go home and think.

When I get back to the chalet I go straight for a drink, I get the vodka bottle out and sit it on the table in the dining room. I pour myself a glass, knock it back. Then another and another. My mum comes in and sits down next to me. "What's the matter Cole? This isn't like you. Normally you are so excited to see us that you can't stop talking. You've been sat in here on your own for over an hour. Tell me what is bothering you?"

"You wouldn't understand mum. Dad and you have this amazing life and you love moving from one country to the next. I love it too, but I don't think it's enough for me anymore. I'm not getting any younger and what if I find the woman of my dreams and she doesn't share my visions, my goals. What if she can't do long distance? What if she doesn't want to live here for four or five months a year? What happens to me then? Do I stay single for the rest of my life? How did you and Dad make it work?"

"Wow, that's deep, Cole. It was hard when I first met your dad, he had only just opened this place and he had to be over here for maybe ten months and then home for two. We had a long chat about it when we realised that our relationship was worth too much to throw away and we worked hard at it. It was really hard; travel wasn't as good back then as it is now don't forget. I came out here as much as I could and your dad came back for a week here and there. When we knew that we would be together forever, I gave up my job so that I could support him and we could become partners in everything."

"So you gave up what you were doing for him. Do you ever regret it?"

"No, at first it was hard and sometimes I would throw it in his face when he was working late and I was on my own in the evenings and didn't know anyone. But it made me get off my bum and go and meet people and start doing my own thing. I started working at the hotel and it was me that suggested the chalets about fifteen years ago. I was involved in the design and build of them – my project if you like. I am invested in this business as much as I am invested in my family."

We sit there for a while not saying anything. "What happened Cole to make you think like this? It's not like you, you're always so positive ... so in control of your emotions and know exactly what you want out of life."

I pour us both a glass and tell her all about Arianna and how amazing she was and how I ruined it because I couldn't think past the ski resort. I told her about how she came to see me to tell me she wants to try a relationship with me and she saw Bianca hugging and kissing me.

"Ah I see, so she ran off crying and you're upset that she thinks you're a player."

"Yes and I'm upset that I didn't make sure that I had a means of contacting her. I really screwed up mum and I hate myself for it." I drink my drink down in one and fill it up again.

"Losing yourself in the bottle is not the right way either Cole. Drink tonight and then when you are feeling better tomorrow we can start working on a plan. There is always a way to get her back. Always!" She leans across and kisses me on the head, just like when I am sick or something. It makes me smile, it feels so familiar.

I watch her walk out of the room and then I drink myself into oblivion.

SUNSHINE

It has been so busy since we got back from Austria, we only had a week to get ready for Christmas, we are not doing that again, ever!

I am so happy Arianna has agreed to come over for Christmas Day, it means they won't be on their own and we can all keep an eye on her. I know she isn't doing well since she got back from the holiday. This situation with Cole has really affected her badly. Kat said she saw her the other day and she has lost a little bit of weight. Her ankle is still a little bit sore but she's not eating and is feeling very depressed. I don't blame her, although we did warn her it was just a holiday fling.

I am at mum's just putting away the groceries for Christmas when I decide to have a cup of tea. I am resting my feet on the chair and drinking my tea when my phone rings. It's a number I don't recognise, but I answer it anyway.

"Hello, Sunshine speaking."

"Hi Sunshine, please don't hang up."

"Who is this?"

"It's Cole, please don't hang up."

"What do you have to say for yourself Cole? Nothing you have to say is of importance to me." I go to hang up and then my curiosity gets the better of me. "OK, you have five minutes before I hang up."

"Thank you so much Sunshine. I need to tell you a little bit about me for you to understand how I feel about Arianna."

"Four minutes and fifty seconds and counting …"

"OK, I deserve that. First of all I want to explain that the girl Arianna saw me with is my sister. She is …

she is very demonstrative." He laughs. "She wasn't due until the Saturday but she turned up early with my mum and dad too. What Arianna saw was my sister hugging me and giving me a kiss as she hadn't seen me in a couple of months."

"I wanted Arianna to tell me that she wanted to try and make it work, I wanted that more than anything. I was upset when she didn't turn up; I was hoping she would change her mind. What you have to understand is that I live for my work. I know that sounds stupid because I teach people how to ski, but it's more than that."

He goes on to tell me about his mum and dad and how they own the resort and how they have a hotel in Bristol and he has set up the travel agency for his sister to take over. This is all he's ever wanted, but after Arianna left he realised that he wants more.

"Ok, so how did you find me? I know you didn't have any of our numbers because Arianna told us on the bus."

"Well, I looked up your reservation details at the hotel and then I saw your mobile number as you had booked it. I hope you don't mind me ringing you, but I just didn't want Arianna thinking that I was only after a holiday romance. I really like her Sunshine and I want to come over and see her again."

"I don't think that's a good idea, Cole. She took everything really badly and I don't think she has started to recover yet."

"I want a chance to tell her how I feel. Do you want to stand in the way of that?"

"It's not up to me Cole. Let me think about it and I will ring you back. This is a lot to take in."

When he has hung up I ring Kat and ask her to come over to help me decide what is the best thing to do. Should we give him the chance to explain himself? Should we be the ones to stand in the way of something that could be beautiful? Should we leave it alone and let Arianna get over it and move on to someone who can give her the stability she so desperately craves?

11 BINDING

ARIANNA

Its Christmas morning and I really don't know what to expect. I've never been for Christmas dinner anywhere else before. I decide to just go with the flow and enjoy the day. I need some lighthearted fun in my life after the last week.

I get mum up and help her to get dressed, then we drive over to India's house. We are the first to arrive and once mum is settled in the lounge with the remote control for the TV, I go and offer Sunshine help with the dinner.

We talk about Christmas and what the kids got from Santa. Cruz was so excited he got an Xbox One this year. "How are you feeling these days Arianna?"

"I'm not too bad, mum is keeping me busy. My ankle is getting better, thank god! I'm looking forward to today though, it will be good to get together with the girls and we can start planning our next trip."

After we have prepared some of the vegetables

Sunshine asks me to set the table in the dining room. She has a beautiful red tablecloth with a white runner down the middle of the table. In the centre of the table she has a silver candelabra which has red candles in it. I light them and they give a warm glow across the table. There are so many people coming for dinner we will be lucky to fit around the table.

There is a separate table for all the kids in the lounge, so they can all sit together and the dining table is extended so it's huge. It reminds me of the dining table in the chalet, I smile and then shake my head. I don't want to remember anything about it, Cole has tainted my memories of that holiday. I can feel the tears pricking my eyes. How I wish things had turned out differently. I had been so excited going to see him to tell him that l was willing to give 'us' a go and then *bam* it felt like he ripped my heart out. I have never been so upset over a bloke before.

I push it to the back of my mind. I know the girls will be talking about it today, but I'll be fine, as long as I can get through the day without thinking about him. When I go home it will be a different story.

The girls start arriving and we all sit in the kitchen with Sunshine and drink prosecco while talking about Christmas. We are having fun when Sydney asks me "Have you heard from Cole?"

The girls are all looking at her and trying to get her to shut up. "No, I didn't give him my number … just a holiday fling remember!"

"I know, but maybe it would have been nice to have spoken to him, given him a chance to explain himself."

"Why? So he could tell me more lies and try to find his way into my knickers again. That's all he wanted … nothing more. Everything else was just an act; he didn't mean any of it. I was gullible enough to believe him; I never thought I would be so stupid. If I just call it a holiday fling then it doesn't hurt so much." I wipe the tears.

"Don't cry hun," Sunshine hands me a clean tissue and pats me on the shoulder. "Don't you ever think that you did something wrong. Sometimes though there are explanations for these situations."

"It doesn't matter though, he doesn't have my number and I am not ringing to speak to him. What if it was true? I am not a fool Sunshine. I just want to have a good Christmas and then in the New Year I can start afresh. No more one night stands; I just want stability in my life."

Sunshine stands up and starts getting everything ready for dinner. "You can all go into the dining room for dinner. Kat can you come and help me please?" We all pile out of the kitchen and into the dining room.

Kat stays with her and I overhear her say "Sunshine, I'm not sure this is a good idea."

"Shh, she'll hear you. I promise Kat it will be fine. Trust me!"

I wonder what they're talking about. When I walk into the dining room Molly asks me "So Arianna, did you get anything nice for Christmas?"

We spend the next hour talking about Christmas presents and eating out dinner. It's gorgeous, even mum likes it and she can be fussy. She doesn't feel great so Xavier helps upstairs to lie down. When he comes back in the room he starts to clear away the dishes.

The doorbell rings and India says "Who the hell is that at the door? It's Christmas Day; everyone we know is here already."

We all laugh at her, then I hear Sunshine shout "Arianna, can you get the door, I am just taking the pudding out of the oven."

"OK, I'll get it." I walk down the hallway and open the door. I'm surprised I don't pass out. It's Cole.

"Happy Christmas, Spunky!" I close the door in his face and lean up against it. The tears flow down my face. What is he doing here? Why is he ruining Christmas by rubbing it in my face?

I hear the letterbox flap being lifted up. "Spunky, please, we need to talk."

"What are you doing here? Why are you here? How? ... How did you know where I was?" I look up and see Sunshine and Kat stood there looking at me. They both have their fingers crossed.

"Arianna, you need to give him chance to explain. I've spoken to him and you need to hear it for yourself."

"Sunshine how could you interfere like this. I didn't want to speak to him. He's a bastard. You know how upset I've been. Please make him go away."

She walks down the corridor to me and takes me in a hug. "I love you Arianna, I'm sorry." I sob into her chest, she rubs my head.

She goes to open the door and I tense up. "It's ok Arianna, I promise."

I feel her opening the door and I'm so happy she is going to tell him to piss off like he should. He is ruining everyone's Christmas day, not just mine.

"Sorry Cole, come in. I'll give you both some space."

"What? … but Sunshine, no!"

He walks in and closes the door behind him. This is like my worst nightmare, maybe I will wake up in a minute and it will be Christmas morning all over again.

He stands behind me and takes me away from Sunshine and tries to pull me in close for a hug, I struggle. He's stronger than me. He eventually manages to get his arms around me and I stand still, there's no point in moving. "Spunky."

"Don't call me that, you don't have the right to call me that anymore."

"Spunky! Yep it still suits you. I need to talk to you. I'm so sorry; I was so upset you didn't come to see me. I was going to tell you I wanted to try and make it work."

"What for five minutes and then you sought solace in someone else's arms?"

"No" he shows me a picture of him and the blonde. "This is my sister Bianca! She wasn't due until Saturday but she turned up early. I promise. There's more though and I need to talk to you and tell you everything. Please give me one chance. If you don't want to know me after I tell you everything then I'll leave, I promise. I want this to work Arianna; you're all I've been able to think about. I haven't even been to work for days."

I can feel my body relaxing slightly. He feels it too and he hugs me tighter. He puts his finger under my chin to raise my head so I have to look at him. When I eventually look into his eyes I see he is as tired looking as me, his eyes are bright with tears and he looks sad. His eyes always looked alive when I looked into them before.

I hear Sunshine say "You can both go into the play room and talk in there." Then I hear her walk back into the kitchen. I hear the whispers of the other girls asking what is going on.

He opens his arms to let me turn around and then he follows me into the play room. I see there is a bottle of prosecco and two glasses. I will kill her, she obviously planned this, but I don't understand how or why?

I sit down in the arm chair and he sits on the couch. "So, you've got ten minutes Cole and then I'm going back to enjoying my Christmas."

He laughs, 'Well that's five minutes longer than Sunshine gave me." He then tells me exactly what he told Sunshine. He shows me pictures of Bianca with him and his parents.

"Ok, so she was your sister. I accept that, but why didn't you tell me that you managed the hotel and that's why you were doing the lessons every year. I thought you went there to pick up girls and you did it every year and you had a different woman each week."

"I didn't want to tell you because I want someone who wants to be with me because of … well me. Not because I manage the hotel and resort. My dad owns it and it will be mine one day, but it was only after you left that I realised it isn't enough for me anymore. I have never felt as lost as when you left me. I didn't like it, but I thought I would get over it. I didn't."

I shuffle in my seat; I can feel my façade melting a little. I'm still pissed off he didn't tell me, but there's one thing I don't understand. "Why didn't Faye tell me it was your sister when she knew why I was upset?"

"This is Faye's first year with us and Bianca hadn't been over to the resort before then. She was busy with the travel agency and didn't have the time. Faye has never met her before."

I don't know what to say, I feel really bad, but I still don't understand what he is doing here and how he got here! "How did you find me? Why did you come to find me?"

He turns to face me and moves onto the couch next to me, he reaches out and takes my hand.

"I want to try and make a go of our relationship. I really missed you when you left, I know I was upset but I REALLY missed you. I kept seeing you in the crowd but when I got closer I realised it wasn't you. You make me laugh, you are a great listener, you … you are amazing. I don't want to be without you. I want stability with you. Please give me a chance. It won't be easy to start with, but it will get easier and soon it will be our life, tailored to both of us." He takes my hand and holds it to his lips, he gently kisses it whilst staring at my face and looking intently into my eyes.

What can I say? I am stunned. "You mean it? You really want to try and make THIS" I say pointing between him and me, "work. Seriously?"

"I have never been so sure of anything in my life,

Arianna." I know he's serious because he called me Arianna.

I start to cry, I can't control the tears. It's like I've opened the floodgates to my emotions. He moves so that he is kneeling in front of me. "Arianna, please don't cry. I can leave if you don't want me to stay. I'm sorry to have ruined your Christmas." He stands to leave.

"No! Don't leave. Please. You've haven't ruined my Christmas, you've made my Christmas. When I went into the cabin, when you were Santa, I silently wished for us to be together at Christmas. I knew there wasn't a chance, but I wanted to see if Christmas miracles really do happen. I guess they do!"

He leans into me and lifts my chin to look into my eyes. "I really want to kiss you Arianna, please let me kiss you. I've missed your lips."

I nod and he slowly lowers his lips to mine and consumes me, not with passion but with every emotion in his heart. This is home for me. This is just where I want to be.

I don't know how long we sit here for, but soon there is a knock at the door and I can hear the door opening slowly. It's Sunshine. "Are you guys ok in here?"

I nod and say "Yes, thank you Sunshine, I know you played a part in this. Thank you."

"I nearly didn't go along with it because I didn't know how you would react, but I felt that you really needed to hear his side of the story from him."

"Yeah I did, I can't believe he's here." I rub his face and just stare at him. Then I start laughing, nervously. "So I guess this is a good time to introduce you to my mum then."

He laughs, "Yes come on let's go and meet everyone." He takes my hand to help me up and then I pull him through to the kitchen where everyone is waiting to see what happens next.

I am sheepish when I walk into the kitchen, but I come straight out with it. "Mum, this is Cole. This is the guy that I met in Austria and he has come all this way to surprise me today."

He moves towards her and shakes her hand and says "Merry Christmas, you have a wonderful daughter."

"Yes I have," mum says. "She needs to be treated right though so don't think about cutting corners where she is concerned."

We all laugh. The girls then take it in turns to get up and say hi to him and give him a hug. He is then introduced to everyone around the table. I notice they have set another table setting next to mine and he sits down with a smile on his face.

I can't believe he is really here ... with me ... in

this kitchen, on Christmas Day. I look around at everyone sitting, eating and generally having fun. This is my family, right here.

THE END

.... Or is it?

EPILOGUE

ARIANNA

So Christmas is well and truly over and what a Christmas it was. After Cole turned up at India's house, we spent every day together until the day before New Year's Eve. Cole had to go back to Austria as New Year is a big celebration over there and they were having a large number of guests staying in the resort.

Obviously, he asked me to go with him and I did. It was manic, really busy but so much fun. We got to party on New Year's Eve and when the clock struck twelve, I found myself in Cole's arms, just where I belong.

I love him more than anything and I don't know what I would do without him. We have had a lot of time apart as I had to come home early in January to look after mum, who, unfortunately, took a turn for the worse. Cole had to stay behind to wrap everything up and get ready for the Easter season, but he did come home at the end of March when mum died.

The night before she died, she spent a few minutes

whispering something to him, he won't tell me what and she didn't tell me what she'd said either. She told me that she was finally happy that I was going to have some stability in my life and that she knew he would make me happy. He has a lot to live up to. He stayed with me for two weeks while we wrapped up her estate and decided what to do with the house and everything. My brother told me to have the house as I had been the one to look after her in the last couple of years. I still have it, but I'm thinking of selling it one day soon.

It's Easter time now and we are in Austria getting ready for the Easter rush, although it hasn't really calmed down here since we came back. I gave up my job in the bank because I want to spend the time travelling with Cole. We have our own chalet and it is really beautiful, it sits far away from the tourist cabins and we have a lot of privacy.

The Sunshine Girls are flying over to be here for Easter with their families and I am so excited, I can't wait to go and collect them from the airport later today.

"Morning Spunky, have you been awake long?" Cole asks as he places small kisses along my collar bone.

I love it when he does that. "A little while. I am so excited about seeing the girls again, I just can't sleep."

He laughs. "It's not that long since you saw them. What time are you collecting them?"

"Two o'clock this afternoon. I'm bringing them

straight back here and then I'm going to cook dinner for everyone tonight. You'll be around won't you?"

"I wouldn't miss it for the world. You always light up when you talk about them and I know how happy they make you."

He goes to work and I drive out to the airport to collect the girls. "Hey Sunshine, how was the trip over?"

"Let's just say it wasn't as eventful as it normally is." She nods her head over to Molly and India when she says that, they must have behaved themselves because Molly's grandkids were on the flight.

I giggle and then make sure that everyone is safely in the transfer bus before driving them back to the resort.

For three days we ski, laugh, cry, eat and drink. It's perfect and I know that I am the happiest that I have ever been. Cole gives me the stability that I have always craved, even though we are constantly between the two countries. It doesn't matter as long as I have him by my side.

Who would have known that our Sunshine Girls trip to Austria would introduce me to the love of my life!

Sneak Peek into the Future

Some on the projects which I am working on to look out for in 2016!

Swan

It's ironic that her name is Lily Swan, because she's always felt like the Ugly Duckling. The one that nobody wants ...

Would you change yourself for a man?

Would you consider surgery to get the man you want? She did ...

Little did she know, it was the best decision she ever made .....

Sunshine in Amsterdam

Can true love be found in the most erotic city in the World? This is a story of six wonderful women who travel around the Cities of Europe having fun and living life to the fullest. Join the Sunshine Tours to find out!

Sweet Girls of Whiskey Sour

Zephyr Knight is trying to make something good with her life. She's the first her family to go to college.

To make ends meet she joins 'The Sweet Girls of Whiskey Sour,' little would she know, by doing so she would make lifelong friends.

This is 'her' story of self-discovery, heartache and never ending friendships.

KRISSY V

ABOUT THE AUTHOR

I know that most of you know about me so these are my other books that I have written:

Till Death Us Do Part Series

Till Death Us Do Part – The Trilogy in one book
To Have and To Hold – Book 4 Standalone
For Richer or For Poorer – Book 5 Standalone

My One Regret

Sunshine Tours
Sunshine in Madrid
Sunshine at Christmas

Christmas Novella
A Taste of Christmas Dublin Style

Anthologies
Love Reborn
When Destiny Calls

Keep your eyes on my facebook page:
www.facebook.com/authorkrissy.vas

Keep your eyes on my blog page:
Authorkrissyv.wordpress.com

Made in the USA
Charleston, SC
05 November 2015